GEORGE

XAVIER'S HATCHLINGS BOOK 4

KATHI S. BARTON

This is a work of fiction. Names, characters, places, and incidents are products of the author's imagination or are used fictitiously and are not to be construed as real. Any resemblance to actual events, locations, organizations, or persons, living or dead, is entirely coincidental.

World Castle Publishing, LLC
Pensacola, Florida
Copyright © Kathi S. Barton 2022
Paperback ISBN: 9781956788648
eBook ISBN: 9781956788655
First Edition World Castle Publishing, LLC, February 28, 2022
http://www.worldcastlepublishing.com

Cover: Karen Fuller
Editor: Maxine Bringenberg

Prologue

Long ago, at a time when all creatures roamed the earth as only their true selves, working with and helping humans in whatever way they could. Where magic was celebrated. And dragons darkened the skies every day. It was then man figured out there was magic in the dragons and hunted them to almost extinction.

"I'm afraid there is no hope for us." No one made a sound as their leader continued. "Once the humans found out about us and what we can do for them dead, we were doomed. I'm so terribly sorry."

Coop looked around the room. There were so few of them now he could easily count them.

When he had been younger, thousands of years ago, there would not be enough room for all of them to share this room. Now they were down to having a quarter of them share the space because so many, his own wife included, had been murdered so needlessly. Coop was saddened by it all. Turning to leave the large cave, he was stopped by his brother, Xavier.

"The boys, they are well?" He nodded and smiled. Coop felt it all the way to his heart, a place that had been dead for so long, it seemed. "You have the spell? You are going to use it on them? I so wish I had thought of this before my own family was taken from me, Coop. You are a brave man and a good father."

"Thank you. And I shall use it tonight. It is the only way to save them." Xavier nodded, his own heart heavy with the losses they had suffered. "You know I would have shared should I have had it sooner. I am so sorry, brother. All of my heart, it's sorry for you."

"I know that. I do. But they are all gone now. My other half, my children. Killed for things not fair to our kind." Coop knew all too well. "Ava was a good woman, Coop. A good woman and mother to your sons. She will be missed forever."

"Aye, in my heart and those of my sons." Xavier stood there for several seconds, and Coop told him he must go. "They're awaiting word on what is to happen with us all."

"One more thing, if you please. It will not take but a second. I have left them all I have. It is where you keep them hidden away, the boys. Deep within the cave, it's all there." Coop asked him what he meant. "I cannot go on, brother. I cannot. There is too much grief in my heart for me to live. I have left my things for them there. They might survive this, with the magic you have to give to them. And if so, they'll need more than you have to help them."

"Xavier, please, you mustn't do this. They'll miss you as much as I." Xavier nodded and said it had begun. "You can come and stay with my sons. You'll live with them in the caves, and they'll care for you."

"Nay. I cannot. I must go. Just tell them I love them. With all of my heart." There would be no stopping him once his heart was made up, Coop knew this, but it made his heart no less full for it. "Goodbye, my brother. Take care you are not caught by the humans."

Coop made his way back to his hidden

cave and sat before the fire. The boys, he knew, were resting, their bodies getting stronger daily with their age. Soon they would be as big as him, dragons of worth and size. When his eldest son came to him, his eyes full of fear, Coop knew it was well past time he did what he had been practicing. The magic would keep them safe.

Gathering his sons, six of them of varying shades of blues and greens, he asked them to have a seat. He had a story to tell them. It was not a story, not truly, but a tale that would, hopefully, keep them safe.

"A witch told me once of a great magic only few can do. It takes a loving heart and a strong dragon to make it work. I have asked her, and she has told me how to make it so. In this magic, it will keep you all safe from the humans." They nodded, each of them knowing it was a human blade that took the life of their dear mother. "I will perform this upon you, each of you at the same time, and give you some magic you will use when you need it. This magic, strong and powerful, will let you roam with the humans, and they'll not know your true self is just below your flesh."

"You mean we'll be humans as well?" He nodded, then shook his head at Cooper, his oldest.

"I don't understand, Father. Will you explain?"

"Yes. The magic I will give you will let you change into your true self when you are alone. But when you are out in the world, you will need to be a human. A man." Cooper looked at his brothers, then back at him as he continued. "With this magic, I will also give you a gift. Something you will need to keep yourself safe should they find out. A stronger armor than any other dragon before you, as well as the same immortality you have now, as man or dragon."

Hudson stared at him for long moments. He was the thinker, and if he could think of a reason for this not to work, he would voice it loudly. He was much like his mother in that. She would be the first to say when she did or did not like something. And the first to say the plan was perfect. He only hoped she would have approved of this.

"I think you are very smart, Father, to try and keep us safe. But I can only think this will not work on you. Or is that your plan?" The boy was much too smart, Coop thought. "If you change us, who will change you?"

"There will be no one to change me, son. I will.... It is my wish to join your mother in this earth." He watched them, seeing if they understood the love he had lost when she was murdered. "Giving you this magic, it will be something I can tell her I've done for her sons. You know as well as I that she loved you more than anything on this earth, including herself."

"She died saving us." Coop nodded at Lincoln. "I'm not happy you're going to die, Father, but I understand wanting to be with Mother. I miss her more every day."

"As do I." He looked at his sons, all of them growing into dragons of worth. "I must have an agreement from you all. Even if one of you does not want this, it will not work. I would say you should think on this hard. For once I have given this to you, there will be no going back."

"I wish to have it." He knew Cooper would be the first. Not that he did not love his father, but Cooper would see things in a way most would not. To not have this done would mean a certain death for them all. Dragons were too valuable dead not to be hunted for all time. "I will do whatever it takes to make sure you are proud of me as well."

"I am already, Cooper. Forever."

The others nodded too. They were ready for this as much as he was dreading it. Because once he started the process to change his sons into men, he would begin to die. It would take all he was to change them.

Standing up, spreading his wings out behind him, Coop told them about the things their uncle had left them. They knew where the family jewels were, the things their mother had left them as well. Once they were standing, their bodies strong and healthy, he felt his heart swell and break for what he was about to do.

"I, Cooper Manning, of the Manning Dragons of the earth, give to my sons, Cooper, Hudson, Lincoln, Lucas, Tristan, and Xavier, all I am. Each of you will take a part of the earth with you when you are converted. The part of you that is unique in all ways will be strengthened and enhanced. You will be immortal, forever, and those you take to your hearts will be as well." His sons bowed before him when he told them to. He said the words over them that would change them to men. Coop could feel his body shutting down, his heart beating a little less. But he had one more thing he wished to bless them with, and held himself upright to give it from his own dying heart. "One day, true love will come to you. And you will have more than you have ever known. It will fill you in ways you cannot ever imagine.

Love will be yours for all times. For only then will you become a true dragon, a Manning Dragon."

~*~

Cooper sat with his brothers while their father lay dying. His heart was weak from what he had done, and it was tearing him apart. Father was weak, yes, but he continued to tell them tales of their mother, of their adventures when they were only small dragons. They were going to be alone soon; their father was so close to joining their mother it hurt Cooper in ways he had not expected.

"What shall we do with his body?" Cooper looked at Tristan and asked him what he meant. "He will not be able to lie here. If the humans were to find him, they would surely cut him up into pieces. I do not want that for him. We were never able to bury Mother in the proper way after what they did to her."

"We could burn his body." Cooper wondered how it would work when Hudson continued. "His scales will be worthless to them should they come upon his body. The magic he held within him also will be useless to them. He will be nothing more than a carcass. They'll leave alone."

Burn his body. It was something to think about. But he did not want to, not while he was still breathing, his body still alive. When he laid his head upon his father's chest, hearing his heart beating slower and slower, Cooper wondered what his father would think if he knew the magic he had given them had not worked. They were all still as dragons.

"He gave his life to keep us safe. But it did not work." No one said anything to him as they each watched their father. "Dragons such as we are, we'll be hunted and killed by the humans. There is nothing we can do but wait for them."

"We will survive if we stay here." Cooper told Xavier they would have to leave eventually. "To feed and to fly, yes. But perhaps we could do it only at night. To keep to the skies and not let them see us."

"They know we are about and will have spies out looking for our lairs. We will have to kill any man should he come for us, and still, we will not be safe. We are, after all, dragons who have a great deal of magic."

Cooper stopped breathing. Cooper did not hear his father's heart and knew it was at an end. He was quiet for a bit longer, waiting, hoping for just one more beat, one more sound that would mean he was still alive. But there was nothing. Their father was dead. Sitting up, he told them he had passed from this world into the next.

None of them had ever seen a dragon die before. Their mother had been dead when they found her. Each dragon they had come upon when they were out had been dead long before they found them, their bodies stripped of every part, so they resembled less of a dragon than just a pile of bones.

Their scales were used for roofs for their homes and for shields. The very meat of them was roasted and stored away so it could be used for medicines and potions. Hearts were cut up and dried, then ground into a powder to use for other things the humans would use to keep them from sickness, as well as magic to have a grand garden and trees heavy with fruit. The only part that would be left was the bones, and sometimes even those were carried off and used for something. Cooper hated all humans.

"We will do as suggested by Hudson. It is the only assured way we can—"

Before he could finish, he felt the stirring of the earth. It shook so hard it knocked each of them off their feet. As they lay there, terrified someone was coming for them, their father appeared before them.

His body was still aground. But instead of dark in death, he was brilliant in light. Faeries, thousands upon thousands of faeries, seemed to be covering him. Before Cooper could tell them to stop, to leave him alone, Father spoke.

"I love you, my sons." Each of them nodded, fear almost something he could touch. "I will now and forever join my true love, your mother. I must warn you, when you find your other half, and you will, you will have to be careful of the slayers. They will know what you have found by the magic you both will share. My sons, you will leave this place and take your place among men. Becoming someone I will be proud of."

"Father, the magic didn't work. We're still dragons." Cooper felt shameful to say a thing like that to his father. To tell him his sacrifice had not worked. "We will be hunted and killed."

"Nay, you only need to think of being your other half. Becoming a man is simple. The same when you wish to be your true self." Cooper was not sure what that meant, but his father continued before he could ask. "Go now, before men come here. The magic to hide me will draw them here. Be safe, my sons, and know I love you more than I do any other creature on this place."

Cooper stood then, the faeries still working, taking the body of his father apart. But as he watched, he could see they were not doing anything but preserving his body. Faerie ropes were all around him, and strings of magic were wrapped around him like a cocoon. It made him invisible to all. As Cooper stood there, his brothers beside him, he knew that, like him, they mourned the loss of yet another parent.

"You are the eldest." He nodded to the faerie when she asked. "We have a gift for you. For all of you, but you will receive the most. Your father was a great man, your mother a queen among her people. We wish to bestow upon you all your father had."

"My brothers, they will need it as well. I should like to share." She smiled at him and bowed. "What have you done with his body?"

"He is being prepared to be moved. We will make a grand garden upon him. Flowers will be there for all to see, but only a few will know a dragon is there with his other half, his love." He nodded. It was as it should be. "You will take this gift? You will share, but as I said, you will get more than the others."

"I don't care. Please, just do what you must so we can hide." She nodded again and touched her fingers, small, tiny ones, to his forehead. Then she did the same to the others before coming back to him. "It is done. You have shared it with us?"

"I have, Lord Cooper. But you must leave here now. There are humans coming. The magic we used to do this thing has given them cause to come here." He nodded and looked at the ground where their father had been. "He is safe. Just as your mother is now. Go, before they find you here and murder you as well."

He thanked her for her help and left. The exit from this part of the cave was hidden so well only they knew about it. As they made their way into the night, he thought of the human inside of him, and the pain of it took his breath away. In seconds, he was down on his knees. Whatever was happening, he was surely going to die.

"You're a man." He looked up at his brothers as they began to transfer to men themselves. "We'll be safe now, all of us. We'll be humans for them until we can find a place where we can be ourselves."

"I don't think that's ever going to happen again." Hudson nodded and held his head tightly as he did so. "We will need to train ourselves in their ways. Become what they are. But never monsters."

"No, never." They made their way to a building; any would do for now. Hudson, like him, was staggering a little, but they were getting stronger as they moved. He turned to look at him as they were settling in the empty shell of a house. "We will need to buy things, houses and such."

"Yes. But tomorrow. I am too tired to think beyond how much we have lost." Hudson and the others agreed. "When the humans are gone from our cave, we'll go and find what Father was telling us about earlier, about the wealth that will keep us safe."

"I only hope there is a great deal of it. I don't know how to work, much less walk around like they do." Cooper told Xavier, the youngest brother, they would soon learn. "I hope so. I hope so."

He did as well. It was going to be hard enough for them to learn to eat and dress like humans, much less get around. Cooper hoped this worked. For he was as afraid as he had ever been in his life.

~*~

After a time, thousands of years, each of the dragons turned into men, forging their way into a world that was so different than the one they had been born to it seemed a different planet. But survive, they did.

Having their mates come to them, children born to all of them, gave them hope. A small and fragile thing after such hardships they were born to. Cooper became, as his father had been before him, the king of dragons—his mate, Carson, their queen. It had been and still was a time for celebration. To this day, they commemorated often and hard at each new birth of the dragons turned men and women.

The others, his brothers, prospered too, finding their other halves, making their magic stronger for having their love. They worked hard in keeping everyone safe and well fed, humans or other dragons. No one, not anyone in need, would have ever been turned away from their help. The Manning Dragons, true to their father and mother, became the most powerful dragons ever born.

Of the six sons, Xavier's sons, four hatchlings, and two humans moved far away to be the next generation of Manning dragons who would open their hearts and doors for all creatures. Even the sons of their heart, the two human born men, carried a powerful magic. They used it, with their brothers, to help as many creatures as possible, humans and dragons alike, to live in the ever-changing world. To help them not only succeed but to perhaps help someone else when they needed it. These boys, now men, have stories to tell.

Chapter 1

Imp didn't move when they were all told to sit on the floor with their hands on their heads. She wasn't going to do anything until the time was right. Knowing that the three men and a woman were robbing the bank on a Friday morning told her they were stupid anyway. Only a numb-nuts would rob a bank that early in the morning after all the money had been put in the armored truck and sent out.

"Who's in charge?" She supposed she could have pointed out it was the dead man on the floor of his office, but she kept her mouth shut. "I asked a question, and I want you to answer."

Imp wondered why he thought the lady wearing her slippers and a hairnet would be working in the bank. She was the elderly lady that came in once a day to check on the balance of her account. And every day, Imp or one of the other tellers working there would tell her there was nothing in the account that she'd have to wait for her social security check to hit. There were five or so bucks in the account, but they never told her that. Mrs. Shelby would take that, and the account would be closed. She'd not get her checks at all if she did that.

Working here was a good way to make some money. Usually, there wasn't any kind of stress. But Imp had no desire to get shot up when she had more important things to do today. Like breathing and having all her blood stay where it was.

"You. Do you work here?" The lady sitting next to her on the floor, Mary Roberts, shook her head. She did, as a matter of fact, work right beside Imp, but when she turned to her, telling the man Imp worked there, Imp thought about never working for her again. If it was to come up after this, she reminded herself. "I want you to get me the manager."

"You already killed him. And if you're going to ask me to open the safe, I can't do that either. You killed the only person that can do that for you." He put the gun at her forehead. "You kill me, and that will definitely not get you any answers. I don't know the combination any more than you do. They don't let us have it as part-timers."

"Why?" She waited for him to say why what, but when he didn't, she finally had to ask him. "Why don't they give it to part-timers? Don't they think people want something out of the vaulter when they come in?"

That was the third time he'd called it a vaulter like it was some gymnastic jump or something. Instead of correcting him, she told him what she knew. That they didn't want anyone that wasn't full-time knowing the combination in the event of the bank being robbed.

"That's just stupid." She didn't tell him she thought robbing the bank was stupid, but he seemed to not care what her opinion was. So when he got up to pace, she didn't move. It was becoming harder and harder to sit still. Imp had been on her way to the bathroom when the people had shown up. Now she really had to pee. "We had this place all ready to be robbed, and now it's not going the way we want."

Again, she had plenty to say to that but prudently kept her mouth shut. Turning to her again, he asked her what was in the drawers they were to use.

"Nothing. I mean, you came in right before we were to open and killed the bank manager right away. He hadn't gotten out the drawers we were to use." Imp nearly screamed when someone spoke to her right by her ear. "Who is that?"

"I'm not going to tell you my name, you moron." She nodded at the man, hoping the woman who had spoken would understand that she meant her. The woman spoke again.

You have the power to end this. Why haven't you? Imp asked her what she was talking about, knowing full well what she could do. *You are very powerful, Imp Perkins. Just stomp your foot, and the police will come in and gather up the idiots. They are, too, as you've noticed.*

I just got my life together here, and I'm not going to do something to jeopardize that. I don't know what people will think if I suddenly just make everyone within a mile fall on their asses. It'll come back to bite me in the ass, and I think you know that, whoever you are, as well as I do. The laughter had her smiling. It was just like what she thought the word mirth would sound like if the dictionary had sound. *You should know, if you're aware of me, that I'm not going to cause trouble when I don't have to.*

He's going to kill everyone in that bank. Can you live with that? She told the voice that she could. *No, you can't. You have a tender heart, and you'd hate for anyone to be hurt. That's why you ran here a few months ago.*

If you know so much, why the hell don't you fix this? I'm assuming you're as capable as I am. She told her she was but wasn't allowed to interfere with humans. *And what makes you think I can? Answer me that? Maybe I can't either.*

Ah, but you can. Do you know why? Because I know just what you are. Imp wasn't sure she was telling her the truth or not. She had no idea what she was or the power that she could wield. *If you do this for me, I'll not only tell you what you are but also where you're from. That would be worth it, right?*

I don't like you very much right now. She told her who she was. *Well, Winnie Manning, not only do I not like you, but I don't care for your name, either. I'm reasonably sure you're not related to the dragons by the same name. Sounds petty, I know.*

Standing up, she was told to sit down. Instead of following orders, she touched the man with her fingertips and said, "Freeze." He looked, for all appearances, just like a man standing still. However, every organ in his body, including his heart, was frozen solid.

Taking his gun from his fingers, she shoved him to the floor. Turning to the other people that had been sitting in the bank with her, she told them to go to the bathroom. However, they just sat there.

"Get your asses in the bathroom before the next guy comes out here and starts firing at you." They moved then. The three other tellers were moving quickly, and she closed her eyes. "Christ, they'll hire anyone."

Winnie laughed but didn't say anything until she was headed toward where the vault was. *There is a man to your right. He's looking toward where you're coming from. When I tell you, you can move.* She waited, and when Winnie said now, she came around the corner and fired twice, hitting him in the head both times. *Good shot. The other two men are in the backroom trying to find the combination to the vault. They don't have any idea that you killed the other man. They're making enough noise to wake the dead in there.*

Entering the room, she was shot once in

the shoulder as soon as she fired on the first man. Killing the second man, she sat down on the floor and tried to work her way through the pain. Winnie asked her if she was all right.

Sure. Getting shot like this is an everyday occurrence for me. You said you'd tell me what I am. What the fuck am I, and how much longer do you suppose I'll live? I've seen enough for several lifetimes. Hell, I've seen several lifetimes. Coughing, a little blood appearing on her fingers, she thought about putting the gun to her head and knew it would only hurt. Nothing would kill her. *Tell me or not. Right now, I'm out of here.*

I'm afraid that's not possible. Imp asked her what she was talking about. *You leaving there. I mean, you could try, but they'll hunt you down. The police already think this is an inside job. If you flee, they'll put out an all-points for you, and since there are four dead men that you killed, they'll blame you for that too. It sucks to be immortal and have a couple of life sentences.*

Did you fucking know this before? She said she hadn't, but she could see it playing out that way. Imp heard a noise behind her and put her hands up when she was told to. *Right now, I could gladly hunt you down and murder you.*

You can't, I'm afraid. I'm an immortal as well. And as for your comment earlier, I am a part of the Manning dragons. I'm their protector. She asked her again what she was. *You're an elemental fae. You can also use fire should you wish, even going so far as combining the two. Did you know that?*

Yeah. When you're around forever, you kind of figure things out. I thought the fae were tiny little things that irritate the shit out of you all the time about eating right and shit. Like the faeries do. She asked her if she had a faerie. *I did. A long time ago. He was killed when we were at war for some kingdom. After the way he was killed, no one wanted to come around anymore. At one time, it was thought that killing the faerie that was with someone would kill them as well. It didn't work out so well for them.*

No, I would think not. Winnie told her she'd be at the jail to post her bond. *No worries for that. I don't want to be beholden to you. I'll just hang out there until they get their heads out of their asses, and I'll be on my way. After today, I think I've worn out my welcome.*

The police asked her what had happened, and she told them, even going so far as to show them her badge, that she had to get into the place. After telling them what she knew about the men, which was nothing, Imp ended up telling them three more times before someone decided she might need medical care. Not that it mattered. Once the bullet was removed, she'd mend on her own. But she knew better than to just hop right up. She'd have to fake it for a few days at least.

The hospital was state of the art. Imp could also tell it was new, even to the people working in the emergency room. She was given a workup, blood pressure taken, temp too, at least four times so far. The officer with her was too busy flirting with one of the staff to notice she wasn't handcuffed to the bed as they'd told her she'd be.

Not that she had any intentions of leaving. Imp had figured out that what Winnie had told her was true. She was guilty until proven otherwise. Not that it didn't happen a great deal with humans. People just didn't trust as much as they used to.

Smiling to herself, she looked up when her name was spoken. "You must be Winnie Manning." She nodded at her and came fully into the room. There was a man with her, and she introduced him as Hudson, her husband. "You must be a hell of a man to have to put up with Winnie, I'm thinking. She's been a pain in my ass since she convinced me that killing four men would be no trouble for me. But I do know what I am now, so that's all right too, I guess. Why are you here?"

"I'm your attorney." Imp didn't bother pointing out that she didn't need one—she could well represent herself in anything like a courtroom. "Also, the king of dragons would like to meet you. My brother, Cooper. He wants to thank you for making sure one of his people wasn't killed."

"Debra." Hudson nodded. "She's not a dragon. I think I would have smelled brimstone on her had she been one."

"She's the daughter of one of the people that work in his nephew's household. He's very grateful to you." Imp looked at Winnie when she sat down. "You've done a great service for him, and he wishes to grant you anything you wish. Within reason."

"Death." Hudson looked at Winnie when she laughed. "I don't think my wanting to die is all that difficult for him to do, if he's the king of dragons or some shit like that. Just burn me up or something like that, and I'll be happy. You did say he wanted to reward me, correct?"

"Not by death." He looked at his wife. "How

did you know that was what she'd ask for? You read her mind, didn't you?"

"No. But I've been where she is. Being around forever. Not having anyone around that you can trust. Yeah, I knew that would be something she wanted." Winnie looked at her. "It wouldn't work anyway, even if Cooper did want to do it for you. You're an immortal, just like us. And I think killing you would be a shame since I do think you're the last of your kind."

"Nope, wrong there. I bet you think you're never wrong, but you are in this. It seems my memory is returning to me. I've been alone for so long, I've all but forgotten who I am. I have not just a sister, but a brother too. We don't…what you might call hang out together. Our combined power would be too much for humans to not feel." She asked her where they were. "I don't know where Glacier is, but my brother is in a cave in Yellowstone. He's been there for decades, keeping away from humans. His name is Ignis." Winnie asked her what her given name was. "Imperium. Imp for short."

The meaning of their names hit Hudson first. When he stood up and sat back down, she watched Winnie. Suddenly the room was filled with faeries and brownies. The order was given to make sure that nothing happened to her.

"I'm guessing you understand what we are. Glacier is ice, Ignis fire. And me the power. But you're wasting your time in protecting me. As you pointed out, I'm an immortal the same as you are." Winnie told her what she was having the little people do. "Ah, so you really know what I am then. What am I? You said you'd tell me."

"You're the power that created dragons' breath. And in turn, created the dragons themselves. Christ, you're everything that...wait until I tell my brother. He's going to have a shitfit that we didn't figure this out sooner."

When the two of them left her, she looked at the faerie that landed on her belly. She told her what she was called.

"Well, Jasmine, I'm Imp. Are you in charge of the little people?" She said she was hers to command. "I'm not really into the commanding thing. If I ask you for something and you're in the middle of something else, then you tell me that. I don't want you to be taken away from your regular duties while keeping an eye on me so that I don't run."

"No, my lady. I am your faerie forever. I

will do as you wish when you wish it." Imp told her she didn't want a faerie. "You must have one. If you are not happy with me as your faerie, there are many more that would gladly take the job."

"It's not that. I don't want anyone to get killed while protecting me, or whatever it is you're thinking I might need from you." She said she'd be fine, that with her, she was an immortal as well.

She'd take it up with someone when she was out of there. She no more wanted a faerie than she did people hanging around with her. Imp had a feeling that once she was out of there, Winnie was going to be up her ass for the rest of her life. Christ, Imp thought, she needed a drink.

Chapter 2

Imp looked out the window from her hospital room. Someone had gone to a great deal of effort to make sure there was a view from this room. She thought if she were to be out there, she'd bring all the seedlings and flowers to life just so she could see the garden in full bloom. But that would cause her issues, and she had enough going on right now.

I felt your pain, Imp. Are you well? She didn't turn to see if her sister was in the room with her or not. Imp couldn't feel her power, so they were talking through their link. *Imp?*

I'm all right. Playing it up for the stupid humans. She turned then, looking at her sister, who was standing as an image in the room with her. "I've not seen you in so long. My goodness, you're still as beautiful as ever. Where have you been, Glacier? It's been decades since we've seen each other."

"I've missed you too. I've been here and there. I've just come from seeing Ignis. He's well, too, I guess. Hiding from humans much like I have been. Do you like them any more than you did before?" She said she'd never like them. "Yes, well, you certainly hang out with them a great deal. Not that I care. But just pointing it out."

Glacier moved around the room. With her power, she could see and even touch the things on Imp's side. It was the two of them in the same space that would cause trouble, such as in this room with her. Their power, even just the two of them, was too much. She asked about the smell that was around the room. It took her a moment to remember what she might be talking about.

"The smell in the room. You remember Winnie?" She looked confused for a moment, then nodded. "She contacted me yesterday when I was hurt. Bank robbery gone wrong. Anyway, she is the protector of the dragons now. Did you do that, or did Ignis?"

"I believe it was Ignis. They certainly

needed someone. Humans were too—humans again. They were so cruel to the dragons that he thought they needed protecting. She's a dragon now?" Imp told her sister what she knew. "Ah, so the Manning dragons are still around, are they? They were a wonderful creation, Imp. I do hope you're proud of them. To be still around after all this time. Good for you."

"The king is wanting to see me. Cooper Manning. He's one of the sons of Coop and his wife, Ava." She asked if they'd been the first. "Yes. I didn't get it right up until then. I haven't any idea why I thought the world needed dragons. But weren't they the most beautiful creatures ever when they were in the sky? I miss seeing them."

"Perhaps he'll allow you to see his dragon once you're there." She told Glacier that he wished to reward her. "Whatever for? For getting shot? That isn't right. I do hope you point that out to him."

"He won't grant me what I want." She didn't have to explain to Glacier what she wanted. Had wanted since she'd seen the destruction of her greatest creation. "Winnie could do it, I think. But then, she's been up my ass since the robbery, telling me I can't do this or that. She is still as bossy as the day she was made by you. You should have started over when she gave you lip that first day." They both laughed, knowing that neither of the three could do that.

Imp sat on the bed when her sister sat down wherever she was. They talked about things for a few minutes until the nurse came in to check on her. The nurse wasn't able to see Glacier, so Imp didn't talk to her while she was there. After she left, Imp introduced Jasmine to her. She seemed as surprised as she'd been when a faerie was presented to her.

"My lady Glacier. If you were to tell me where you are, I would gladly send you a faerie that would help you." Glacier laughed and said she couldn't have a faerie unless Imp said it was all right. "But his lordship, the king of dragons, he will want you to have someone. I can ask if you wish."

"No, don't bother. If I were to have a faerie, it would have to deal with my coldness. But, as I said, Imp must approve of a faerie for myself and Ignis. She is the oldest." Imp could tell Jasmine was confused, but she didn't say anything. "Would you wish for me to explain it to you, young faerie?"

"If you would, please?" Glacier turned to her then, and Imp nodded at her sister. "I would not wish to cause you trouble, my lady. I understand how the birth order can make one in charge, so if you would explain to me, I would understand better."

"The three of us were born as triplets, all in the same flower bud of the most extraordinary color." As her sister told the little faerie, Imp reached out for her brother. Ignis had been quiet for far too long, and she suddenly had a need to speak to him.

I've nothing to say at the moment. I'm not busy, but I'm enjoying my quiet time. She told him she missed him. *And I you. I spoke to Glacier today. Or was that yesterday? I'm not sure anymore. She is well too.*

She's come to see me here. I've been hurt by some stupid humans. The king of dragons wishes to reward me for my services in a bank robbery. Why don't humans just work…? Never mind. I know the answer to that. I'd like you to come here, should you wish. I would like to see the three of us together for a bit. Ignis told her he didn't like people. *I know that, but you could just come here so Glacier and I can see you. No one sees her when they come into my hospital room.*

Are you making me come there, little sister? His laughter made her smile. *I shall come for a short visit. Only to appease you. Oh, I do have news too that I have discovered quite by accident. Did you know that the Manning dragons have had children? They're all males.*

Yes, the son of Coop is now the king of dragons. He's the one I was telling you about. He hummed, meaning he was impressed. *I can make arrangements so you could come here to see him should you wish.*

Nay. I am quite content to live vicariously through you. But I will insist that you tell me about it in great detail. He said he'd be leaving in a few seconds. *I have something going on here. Did you know that my cave has all the comforts of home? However, I have heard rustling around, so I wonder if they are looking for other tunnels in this part of my world. I shan't like moving again. I was here first. But I will. Just because they'll want to discover the sites I have in here.* Ignis babbled on about things he might well have thought she knew until he appeared in her room in the same manner Glacier had.

Ignis looked as fantastic as she remembered. He was a wonderful man, and she had missed him. However, this would be the only way she could see the other two. Not being able to hug them was painful, but she could see them and vowed to do so more often. They had done that before, been too close together, and their combined powers caused all sorts of trouble for the earth. They could meet one at a time, but even that was pushing it.

Imp talked to Ignis for a little while longer while Glacier finished up her tale. Then the three of them talked, telling each what they'd been up to as well as how they were getting along. Which, for the most part, was that they were doing well. However, Imp craved the company of people around her, while the other two didn't. It didn't matter if they were humans or other creatures. Her brother and sister would just as soon be alone.

Feeling the magic as it came toward her, she warned the other two that the king was on his way. They didn't leave — it wasn't as if he could see them anyway unless they or she allowed it. But they didn't speak to her any longer.

The short knock at the door had her bidding the king to enter. Imp stared at the man when he entered the room with a beautiful woman. She knew who they were, of course, but she was startled by their beauty. When the woman, her name eluded her at the moment, laughed, she did as well.

"It's not usual for me to be able to see the end product of a creation of mine. Your father was a good dragon, father and friend to all." The man sat down, hard enough that she was sure the chair beneath him regretted it. "I'm sorry for being so blunt. But like my brother and sister, we're not into niceties. How are you, Cooper?"

"You created my father." It wasn't a statement, but she nodded anyway, stretching out on the only other place to sit, the bed. "When Winnie told me you were here, I didn't know what to think. I mean, the stories of you and your family aren't out there for people to know."

"As they shouldn't be. There is more of a connection to you and my family than I think you were made aware of. My sister, Glacier, pretended to be the witch your father was seeing to get the magic to change you and your brothers. I'm sorry I didn't think of that when I made you. Allowing you to change into humans. It might have saved you from losing him as well." Cooper nodded, but she could tell he was overwhelmed. "Whatever you have for me, Cooper, I don't want it. I'm glad to see you, and that is payment enough for whatever it is you think I did the other day. Besides, you should be thanking Winnie—she is the one that bullied me into it."

"She's good at that. My name is Carson Manning. It's lovely to meet you. And I wish to thank you from the bottom of my heart for creating dragons. They're magnificent creatures." Imp looked at Ignis when he said her name. Carson looked in the direction she was. "Is there someone here with us?"

"My sister, Glacier, is there to your right. Ignis is to your left. They're not really here, however. Just visiting." Cooper asked her if they'd all come to have a meal with them. "I'm sorry, but that's just not possible. Our power is too great when combined."

"Then you. And your family the way they are now if they could. I have so many questions. More than I can put into any kind of order right at the moment. I'm sure my brothers will as well. And there is so much we could tell you, I think. I'd love to have you talk to my family about why and how you created us. It must have taken a great deal of magic to have created dragons of such size." She looked at Ignis, then at her sister. Neither wanted to go, but they would, they told her. Glad for their help, she said they were set to release her today, and she'd meet them wherever they wanted. "Good. That's good. I think with you being released, you'd be able to come to dinner this evening. I'll let you know which home we'll hold it at. Also, I don't know if you were aware of this or not, but there will be no charges against you. And you can still work at your job should you wish."

"No, it's time I moved on. I thought I could stay here a bit longer, but things…well, I'm going to be moving on after this talk session." He looked disappointed, then brightened up. She could have looked, she supposed but didn't. She didn't care all that much what he was thinking anyway. She was a good deal stronger than he was. But she didn't care.

After making arrangements to meet up at the house the dinner was being served at, the couple left. While it hadn't taken all that long to talk to the man, Imp had a feeling it was only the start. Glacier left not long after Cooper and his wife did. Asking Ignis what he was thinking about, she was surprised when he answered her.

"Lots of things lately. Mostly about the three of us. I do wonder at times if there was, at any point, someone who could have removed two of us from the same flower. Perhaps that might have...I don't know, Imp—maybe passed the magic to any other fae in the land." She told him that Winnie had thought she was an elemental faerie. "We were supposed to have been, correct? I mean, we would have been able to take care of so many things as a trio. Don't you think?"

"Do you miss working in the fire, Ignis?" He said he had fun with the hot spots around. Making messes that need to be cleaned up. Mischievous things that he got a lot of sport out of. "Do you ever go back to the volcanos anymore? The ones that are dead now? I know you used to love going there for fun."

"I don't do that too much anymore. I do go back and look at the devastation still. Looking for how it was caused. Why so many people were killed. I didn't do all of them. I'm so much better at the control of such things." She asked him if he thought someone was deliberately doing it. "No. No, there are none stronger than the three of us. I think it's just the earth, trying to stretch her wings, so to speak. Are you sure we should be going to this house? Not that I'm worried for any of us, but it seems we're going to be talking about things we did and the mistakes we made in creating dragons. Do you still think it was a mistake?"

"Yes. Not that I would harm them. It was just a whim that I wanted to see great beasts fly. I had no name for them at the time, as you know. I didn't know that humans would eventually harm them to the point of them being nearly gone. I have heard that the best things are made without much in the way of planning. And that was what it was when I decided to do this." He nodded. "I couldn't have done it without you or Glacier — you know that, don't you? I'm not saying you're to blame — it was my idea — but I will ever be so grateful that you helped me do this on a day I was hurting."

"You still hurt, Imp. I can feel that too." She didn't say anything. What did it matter in the long run of things? "You have wished for and tempted death far too many times for me to have been able to ignore it. With so much around you, how could you wish to die?" She asked him when was the last time he did anything alive other than to hide away. "But I do, love. I do live. I enjoy the caves I dwell in. The food that I forage. I know that I have eaten, as well as you, many things that have come to us in one way or another. But I still try things. Marvel at things as well. In the late of the night, I love to go up and watch the sun coming up, so close to it that I can feel her heat. The deeps of the water still hold appeal for me as well. You aren't doing anything like that, but brooding as to why you are still alive after all these years. Find yourself a lover and enjoy him until he begs you for no more. Raise a child. Open a bookstore. Anything but working and working all the time. You've no need for money, any more than Glacier or I do. Enjoy the life we have."

She wanted to tell him that all the enjoyment had been sucked out of life for her. Mostly it was from seeing children she'd never have. To talk to someone that didn't have an agenda or a phone plastered to their face. Imp thought too she might enjoy just sitting with a person who did none of those things, not even to speak about things that were around them. Imp supposed she just missed people being nice.

Being released from the hospital didn't scare away her brother. Since it was still early in the day, she brought him to the place she'd been living, and he laughed at her lack of a computer, as well as a television. Neither of which appealed to her, but she could use them if needed. He told her about his place.

"I have a television as large as…the people on it are larger than life, much like you are to me. There are computers in every room that I use when I think of something. Like the other day, I thought of a man we knew so long ago his face had disappeared from my memories. And there he was, right there on the screen. He'd made something of his life, just as I had told him to do." He told her of other things as well. Things he'd been testing that he'd ordered from the Internet. The man was a wonder. However, she knew he missed her as much as she and Glacier did him. "Well, I should get back. Rest up for tonight. I was wondering something, Imp. What will you do if he asks you to stay?"

"I'm not going to. There is no reason at all for me to stay with these people." He asked her if there was any reason ever for her to stay in one spot. "Yes, I suppose. A man I could fall in love with. A person I'd want to share my hopes with — I have very few of them, to be honest, but to share those things would be nice. But as you've figured out, too, I don't believe there is anyone out there for the three of us. Happiness wasn't something we were able to figure out in the long run, I don't think."

"I don't believe that. I believe in love. I've seen it. I don't like humans, but sometimes them falling in love with something or someone is entertaining." He seemed to think on it for several minutes before shaking his head. "No, I guess you're right. There is no love for us. Sad really. Think of the kind of parents we could have been."

She was still laughing when he left her. Imp decided she was going to do this more often. Just pop out to see her sister and brother and make an afternoon of it. It might chase away the blues sometimes.

~*~

George didn't like the house he'd been living in. It wasn't bad, he knew, just not his style. He supposed it had to do with the amount of time he spent in the home that hadn't made him fall in love with it. Out of seven days at a time, he might well have spent less than ten hours at the house. It had meant that little to him. But this house? Well, he was in love from the moment he'd seen it with his mom. And getting the furniture too had been a boon he never thought to have.

"Are you sure you don't mind using your home for dinner tonight? I don't want you to think just because you're new to the house, you have to hold this for us, George." He told his mom he was thrilled to have people coming over. "I hope so. I know you know how we can get, but I don't know a thing about this woman and her family."

"The family, as you call them, won't actually be here. Not all of them. Something about the power they give off. What do you know about Imperious, or her brother and sister? I meant to ask Uncle Cooper, but he seemed oddly excited about this." She told him she thought it was from getting information about his parents. "Could be, I guess. I've never seen him walking around and rubbing his hands together like he's plotting or something. Aunt Carson is doing the same thing."

He let it go in favor of looking to see what the faeries were up to. The kitchen and the rest of the house had been deep cleaned by them. The windows had been wobbly in that they were old, but they had been reinforced so no air would get into the house that they didn't want. Also, he'd had them remove all the carpets and clean up the hardwood floors. He loved it much better.

George made his way into the study that he'd been spending most of his time in. The fireplace in the room wasn't as large as the one in the living room. However, when asked to have it cleaned, he'd thought it was just brick. Once the faeries were able to get to the heart of it, they discovered the brick had been covering a white front that was made of marble. It was, he thought, the most beautiful thing in the house, next to the skylights in the master bedroom that they'd uncovered as well.

"I was noticing something in your dining room." He nodded at his brother, Hedley, and asked him what he'd found. "Other than it expands like the rest of the houses do, did you know that there were China cabinets in the corners at one time? I mean, it could have been something you've removed, but that doesn't seem like something you'd do. Not with all the other things you left in the house."

"I didn't see that. And none of the faeries mentioned it." He stood up and smiled at Hedley. "There is a great deal of odds and ends I discovered out in the barn. Wanna go out there with me and see if they might have kept them? I'd love to see if we can find them in there."

They were digging through some of the furniture when Hedley found one of the cabinets. There was only one corner that looked as if something slid into the sides of it from behind.

Then they were able to find the two larger ones that seemed to fit on either side of it to form a large corner cabinet. The solid wood piece was heavy, but they had no trouble pulling it out into the sunlight to look at it. While they were getting the last piece out, they also unearthed a box of china and glasses.

"Christ, I'm going to have to come out here and have a thorough look around for a couple of days, I think. I have been meaning to, but just getting the house ready to live in was a chore. Even with the faeries around." Calling for some of the faeries, they cleaned the cabinet up in record time and set it in the house. It fit just as they had thought it would, he was told. "Do you need anything for your home? I mean, I don't know that I can use all this stuff out here."

"I'll take you up on that. I love my house, I do, but it's not homey enough. Mom is going to help me change things around a bit so it'll be more to my tastes." Hedley laughed. "She said I needed a mate and that she'd make it homey. I don't think she's paying much attention to the women our brothers have married. They're no more domestic than I am."

They were still laughing as the dishes, place

settings for twenty-four people, were cleaned and put into the house. There was also a box of silverware that looked like it went with the place settings. Milo joined them as they were pulling out a trunk.

"Christ, look at that. That's the most beautiful bunkbed set I've ever seen. The detail on it is something that had to be handmade." Caleb was with him, hanging onto Milo like he was terrified of being left behind. "Do you like that, son? If so, maybe we can have one of the faeries make one for you. Look at all the animals chasing each other on the head and footboard."

"You can have it, Caleb, if you want it. I don't know who made it or where it might have come from, but your dad is right. It is very nice." Caleb, still getting used to them all, asked what he'd have to pay for it. "Nothing other than to let me see it when it's set up in your room. In fact, after it's cleaned up, we can have the faeries take it to your room tonight."

"I have a bed in there. Can we do it tomorrow? I want to think about how it would fit." Magic was something else he was getting used to. Even though he could have told the boy that the faeries would move it anywhere he wanted, he told him that would be good. "Can I look around? I was looking for a desk. I'll not bother it if you don't want me to have it."

When he walked away, he looked at his brother. Milo was watching the boy with so much pain written on his face that George hurt for him. He asked him if he was doing all right.

"Yes. Better than I am, I think. He's not been to school as yet, but that does worry him. He's healing well, but not fast enough for me. Jamie wants to keep him at home for the rest of his life, of course. But we both know that's not going to be good for any of us." Milo looked at him. "You don't mind about the bed?"

"Not at all. I think it might make him trust us more should he feel like he's part of the family. To be honest with you, Milo, this piece doesn't look a thing like the rest of the house. Do you think?" Milo said it didn't that it seemed newer to him. "That's what I was thinking. However, the detail is done so well I think it looks like it was done by some kind of laser work. But then that's just me."

Their brothers joined them after a bit. They were having so much fun finding things that George was sure they were going to stuff his home with the antiques that had been left in the large barn.

They'd found a spindle crib that looked nice, as well as a couple of rocking chairs that needed to have the bottoms redone. There were several trunks that Caleb wanted one of. He also was able to unearth a box of toys, some of them so rusty that they were a danger, but Snowball was excited to get to work on them.

"My kids, you see. They could ride around in them should we motorize them a bit. Carrying things back and forth too." George told him that was an excellent idea and handed them over to them. "When you have children yourself, sir, I'll gladly give them back to you."

Thanking him, George noticed his dad showed up just as the first one was cleaned up. The man was a sucker for toys—had been all their life. If they got anything special for holidays or just purchased for themself, you could bet their dad would be looking at it to see how it was put together. Then he'd spend as much time as you'd let him playing with it with you.

They were all deep in the barn, finding the parts to some other piece of furniture that had been taken apart to move when they all turned to hear Mom talking. None of them would say a word about what they were doing, but Dad seemed as confused as they were about her coming out.

"What did I send you out here for, Xavier?" Dad paused just long enough for Mom to start tapping her foot. When he remembered whatever it was, he turned to them and smiled. "You forgot, didn't you?"

"Yes, love, I did. But look, they have—" Mom cleared her throat. "Yes. I came out to tell you that dinner is ready and the guests have arrived. I got sidetracked. That's not a good excuse to make everyone wait on us, but that's what happened."

Dad pulled Mom into an embrace. After kissing her soundly on the mouth, he leaned her back so it looked like one of those old movies where at the end of a dance, he would hold her in just a certain way. They were both giggling— yes, he thought, his parents were giggling as they went into the house, the six of them right behind them.

The house smelled great. He wasn't the only one that noticed it, but he was surprised by the different things each of them smelled. George smelled lavender. The other five smelled varying scents of the outdoors. Fresh water. The scent after the rain. Racing to be the first to meet their guest,

George was second. It was Hedley that made them all stop in the doorway just as he came up behind him.

"What happened?" He didn't speak. George looked around his brother, not an easy fete since he was blocking the entire door. "Hedley, what the hell is wrong with you?"

He saw them then, the three people he'd only just recently heard of. Their creators, at least his grandparents'. When he was able to get Hedley to move again, they all came into the room to have a seat. The two that weren't in the room with them but still there were laughing at the only stranger in the room. She was exquisite.

Chapter 3

Imp wasn't sure what the men were wanting from her, so she remained quiet. Not that she didn't answer questions they shot at her like a gun, but she wasn't comfortable with all of them staring at her. It wasn't until the man who'd been introduced to her as George stood up that she felt her inner beast, her magic, seem to calm a little.

"We're scaring her. Well, not scaring, but I'm thinking we can do this in the living room after we've eaten. I don't know if you guys noticed this or not, but there is a heck of a feast going on in front of us, and we're basically too thunderstruck to enjoy it." Uncle Cooper laughed at George. "Seriously, Uncle Cooper. She's been around longer than anyone in this room. I'm reasonably sure she will do as she said she would and answer questions. So, since this is my home, I'm going to have to insist that we give her time to eat. I know I'd feel better dealing with a room full of dragons if I could do it when I'm calmer."

"Thank you. That would be nice." Imp picked up her fork and began eating the salad she'd made herself. "I don't eat meat, by the way. I am an elemental fae, and as such, I don't do meat."

Imp didn't know how to process in her mind that there were two generations at the table with her or that she had been responsible for having them here. There were Coops and Ava's sons scattered like buckshot around the table with their wives. And among them, the youngest son of her creations, Xavier, and his mate were here with his sons and their mates. She did wonder what the first couple would think about all this and knew they'd be so proud.

"She rarely eats anything but sweets." Her brother Ignis laughed when he spoke. "She's just trying to make herself look good. But I can answer the question that was posed to us. It's a short story and won't keep interrupting the meal. The three of us were put into a single flower to be born. I don't know who did it or how that happened, or even if it happened a great deal. But when the flower was too heavy with our combined weight, the flower broke off and dropped us to the ground. It was Imp that was the first to get out. Glacier and I would have been content, I think, to just rest a bit more. Once Imp was out of the flower, she grew to be what she is right now, as did my sister and I. So you see, in answer to your question, no, we were not made by Mother Nature. I think she was created well after we were."

"She was needed." They turned to Glacier, taking a little of the pressure off her, and Imp was grateful. "Once we began exploring anything and everything we could, we decided there was a need for someone to control what was going on around us. Not the faeries—we had nothing to do with them—but we requested of the earth to make a being that would make sure that things were just so for anyone coming around."

"You're older than Mother Nature?" Cooper's face reddened, and he apologized for his outburst. "I'm sorry for that. I don't have any idea why we all, I think, assumed she created the three of you. I'm glad for it. I truly am. I'd not have met my mate without you. Or I guess even had been made."

The rest of the meal was talking about the house that George had purchased from the family. He was quite proud of the place and with good reason. The walls were sturdy, and the way it was taken care of made her think it would be here long after the world changed once again.

When the little boy entered the room, speaking quietly to Jamie, she listened. The boy's pain was fresh like he'd only just bumped his arm. It was Glacier that suggested to her through their link that she help him with the pain. Without thought to what the parents might say, she asked young Caleb to come to her.

"May I touch you?" He nodded but looked a little hesitant. "I shall never harm you, young man. Never will any of the three of us harm a child in any way. But I'd like to see to your arm there if you'd allow it. It will never hurt, what might happen, but it will perhaps make you feel just a little better."

He looked toward his parents, then back at her after they nodded. "I lost my arm because my real parents beat me. I have kidney troubles too." She nodded and looked back at Milo and Jamie before touching him. They both looked worried but didn't stop her from helping him. "Mom told me she can't fix my kidney because it had to be taken out when I was younger. I was shoved down a flight of stairs then, and it broke me up badly."

"And where are these pillars of good parenting skills?" She glared at Ignis when he asked. "I'm sorry. I don't hang out with people much, so my skills with them are terrible. Go on, young man, let my sister see what her magic will do for you."

"You don't know." Imp shook her head at Milo. "But you know that something will happen for him. How does that work, I wonder?"

"I have done this before. Helped a victim of abuse regain some usage of an appendage that has been lost to them. I supply the magic and the body, his body, decides how best to use it. That's what I am, the power. And the reason we can't be all together. The power I have is so great that with a single touch to my sister and brother, we could literally destroy the world. Not as you know it, but annihilate it. Are you ready, Caleb?"

"Yes, ma'am." When she got the wrapping off his shoulder to his elbow, she looked at the stitches there. "My mom worked on me. She tried to save my arm, but it, like my kidney, couldn't be saved. Your hands are very warm, ma'am."

"Imp. Please call me Imp. And your mom did an amazing job, Caleb. She seems to have put a great deal of love into keeping you well." She touched both her hands to his shoulder and could feel the power surging over the young man. Not wanting to overwhelm him or the people at the table, she told them how she'd come to create her first dragon. "I was sad that day. I have been sadder daily since then, but on this day, I was terribly so. The mountain we were living in, the deep cave, had fallen, crushing inside of it the plants and such that I had collected. I could have gotten more, of course, but on that day, it seemed my plans were never going to come to be anything. As I lay on the ground, looking up at the evening sky, Glacier and Ignis laid beside me. This was the last time we would be together as a family, as it turned out. After that, my power, along with theirs, was immeasurable, as humans say."

"Where were you living then?" She told Lincoln they'd been living in the cave the dragons had been born in. The one where his parents had been created. "They were the first then? You decided to create them right there?"

"Yes. On a whim. I wanted to see great beasts flying through the sky. Ones that could, if necessary, care for themselves and, while at it, spread their magic wide and far. I'm sure you do that now. When you fly, it not only shares the magic you were given, but you also lighten the hearts of those that can feel you out there. The dragons did that for a long time before humans started to think of them more as weapons than what they were there for. Their beauty." She watched Caleb as the magic worked over his arm and body. Imp knew the moment his missing kidney was replaced. His other was strengthened as well. Thinking she'd done all she could for him, the magic in her hands needed more. "Your—I guess he would be your grandfather—was the first dragon. I could see him in my mind's eye. See him as he soared through the skies. Finding the right gem, the perfect one that would give him the color I had envisioned, I put my magic into the diamond and created him. A smaller version of him until I could get him out of doors. But he was more than I could have hoped for in seeing him alive."

"The fire was an afterthought." Ignis took over then, telling them how they'd come to give them fire. "Glacier was afraid that as such a large beast—how he turned out when we took him out of doors—he'd not be able to fend well for himself. I don't know why we didn't think they'd be trapped for the very thing we gave them, but as it turned out, I touched my finger to his snout and fire was put into his lungs."

"Not all of them were fire breathers. Some I put some magic in them. Much like you, Hedley and Dover. You can breathe fire, but it's not all you have. Like Ava, I believe you ended up calling her. She was made by Imp too, but it was from a stone of jade. Of course, we didn't know what it was called then, but she was the perfect creation for that particular shade. It hid her well over the centuries and kept her babies safe." Glacier seemed to think of something else and smiled at them. "All the dragons were made from gems. That is why they cry the gems when they are happy or upset. I thought it was a nice touch. Something they could barter with. That didn't work out so well either, as it turned out."

"I thought I'd made a mistake." No one made a sound as Imp pulled her hands from Caleb. "I'm sorry. I didn't know it was going to happen like this, Caleb. But I will give you a bit of magic to make sure no one thinks any differently about you. All right?"

"You gave me back my hand." Imp told him his body had done it. But that anyone that had known him without his hand wouldn't remember him not having the appendage. "But I didn't have it before. You gave it back to me with your magic. Thank you so much, Miss Imp. I don't know —"

When he wrapped his arms around her, she held him to her. Again, it had been much too long since anyone had touched her, much less with so much love. Tears filled her eyes, and she had to close them with the onslaught of feelings. It was Glacier that got her under control by talking her through the amount of emotions that were centered in her body. Letting go of Caleb was perhaps one of the most difficult things she'd ever done.

"I'm going to step outside."

The men were standing as she disappeared. Being outside in the evening air had her gasping for breath until she thought she could take a step. The man standing in front of her when she opened her eyes was smiling at her.

"They're a bit overwhelming, aren't they? I'm George." She told him, really snapped at him, that she knew who he was. That made him laugh for some reason. "If you were to take it down a couple of notches, I'll talk to you. Otherwise, I'm going to leave you out here to be fret over by the faeries. They're practically vibrating the shingles off the house, wanting to come out and make sure you're all right."

"He hugged me." George nodded and told her it was the first time he'd done that to anyone as far as he knew. "People don't just hug like a child does. It's been so long since I've been touched by anyone that the emotions of it got to me. I'm all right now. I think."

"Come with me." She went with him, not even sure why she bothered. Imp had told him she was all right, but he was headed to the barn. "I found a couple of things while we were in the barn earlier today. I think, now that I've been around you, that you might know who did the work on this bunkbed we unearthed. I have a feeling, I have no idea why, that Ignis did it."

She knew her brother had done it the moment she saw it. "He was so bored when we were apart that he began making furniture. For himself mostly, but he did like to take his time with a piece. This one went to a series of woodland creatures that were around him at the time."

Imp touched her fingers to the wood and felt Ignis's love for the project. The back of the barn was calling to her, so she made her way there simply by flying over the stacks and stacks of things piled up.

"You can fly." It was on the tip of her tongue to tell him he was stupid for pointing it out, but she didn't. Her stress level was down thanks to him, and she needed that more than to make a point. "I'm guessing I'll be able to as well."

"There is a dresser here that matches the bed. Also, I believe there might have been a large bookshelf. If it's not here, I'll have Ignis make one for you." He told her he had given the bed to Caleb. "That's a wonderful idea. He will need something like this as he gets stronger. Do you suppose your brother will be—? What did you say to me?"

"I said I have given it to Caleb. He liked it, so that—" She growled at him, and he laughed again. "I said I could more than likely fly too. Wouldn't you think?"

"Why would I think that?" He shrugged. "Don't do that. You'll tell me what you mean by that. Why is it you think you should be able to fly simply because—? Oh no. No, no, no, no. This isn't happening."

"It is. I'm not sorry it is, but I believe we're going to be together for the rest of our days." She pointed out that she could kill him. It was within her power to do so. "For being your mate? Come on, you will have all kinds of better reasons than that if you hang out with me much. I'm a pain in the ass on my best days. Also, very blunt. People hate that about me."

"I didn't come here looking to have a mate. I...I'm not mate-able." He asked her if she'd made that word up. "Of course I did, you moron. I'm much too powerful to be mated to a dragon. I could hurt you. Or your family."

"No, I don't think you will. Any of us. Why are you so set against being mate-able, Imp? Is it me or just in general?" She told him both. "All right. Then let's narrow that down."

"No. No narrowing anything down. Do you have any idea what I am?" He nodded. "You're certifiable. That's what—holy Christ, he saw it. That bastard Cooper, he saw it, or someone told him we'd be mates. I'm going to kill him."

She went past him and into the house, mumbling all the way about men and their fucking way to get into things that didn't concern them. As soon as she found him, Imp slapped the big dragon on the face. He didn't move. Nor did the people around the two of them.

"You knew. When you were at the hospital, you knew that George was going to be my mate." He didn't answer her but did glance over her head to someone behind her. "If anyone moves toward us, I will destroy the lot of you. I'm that pissed off."

"I can see that. However, it's not my family that is behind you, but the queen of the earth, Dawn herself. And she doesn't look any happier than you are at the moment. By the way, I would like to, on behalf of my entire family, thank you for what you did for young Caleb. I'm not sure how that is to work for him when he returns to the doctor soon. But needless to say, we're all thrilled that he's going to have a better shot in this world." Imp turned, ready to do battle with the queen, too, if necessary. She told Cooper she'd only given the strength to Caleb's body, nothing more. "I don't know why you'd think you need to be pissy with me, but I'm willing to help us get to the bottom of it if it makes you feel any better. I did know, yes, but not that it would be George. I'm happy to welcome you to the family. However, I will hold onto that until you're in a much better mood."

"I'm afraid that might take longer than the earth can spin, young Cooper." Dawn sat down on the chair nearest to her. "I'd like to hear, even though I was there, the story again if you'd not mind telling the rest of what you started today. I'm sure that anyone in this room will be glad for the truth behind their beginning." Imp told her she was angry. "You are forever angry, Imperium. Even when you called to the earth for me to be created, you were angry that whoever created the three of you should have taken better care of the earth. The trouble is, there were people there to do the job. But they weren't as good at it as I have been. Now, have a seat and tell these dragons about their beginnings."

She wanted to be angry still. Tell the stupid king where he could shove his help. But she didn't. Imp had come to this home for the sole reason of telling them how they had begun. How, after all these decades upon decades, she still wished she'd done things differently.

"They were good dragons. The best. As was Xavier, your uncle. As you well know." Dawn told the others in the room that Xavier, brother to Coop, had been made to keep the other two company until children were to come along to them. "Then I created him a wife. Then more and more when I could see that without a group of dragons, I'd never get to see them fill the sky as I had dreamed of. Things were so much...I guess quieter back then. I'm still upset about this."

"I can see that." Dawn stood. "I'd love to sit in that lovely living room of yours, George. Do you think we can have some tea and a few desserts? I can provide the sweets if you wish. I know for a fact that Imperium loves lemon curd cakes."

She didn't care for all this information about herself to be spread around to these people. Stomping into the living room, being the last to enter, Imp wondered if she'd have to be nice from now on. Fuck it, she thought. This wasn't her trouble.

"I want to show you something." While Cooper went to get something, she turned to her brother and told him of the bunkbed that was in the barn. Also of the dresser. When he disappeared for a few minutes, he told her that Caleb had the entire set now, as he should have. While she didn't know what that would mean, she was happy to see the glint in Ignis's eye when he talked to the young boy. Cooper came back into the room with a smallish box. "George said this called him to buy it. It was at an auction house, and we believe it's of our mother. Her memories are fading for us all, but I think this is a likeness of her."

"Would you like to see what she looked like then?" They didn't move but stood standing or sitting where they were enough to make her wonder if she'd said the wrong thing. "It's all right if you don't. I was just—"

The room erupted in the people telling her that they did indeed want to see an image of their long-lost relative. Telling everyone to have a seat far back, she was glad to see that the room seemed to understand this was going to be larger than life. As she lifted her arms to the ceiling, thinking of the beautiful dragons of long ago, they appeared in front of her.

"Oh, Mother. Dad." Cooper was visibly upset, but she didn't think it had to do with him being upset with her any longer. "Look at them. They're so beautiful. Not a single scar like I remember them having when I was a hatchling. Do you see them, Xavier? I know you were so young when they were gone. I hope this helps you remember them too."

"It does. It's like they're right here with us." They didn't get up to touch the images, so she made them walk around. They were only memories that she had stored up of them learning to walk, which had brought her such joy that day. The people in the room experienced it as well.

"Your mother, I remember her learning to walk. This was before we gave them fire." Ignis laughed a little as he continued. "Your father, such a large dragon, stumbled around in the forest so much that trees were felled and boulders were broken. But he got it. Taking to the skies together, it was easier than walking. Oh my, the times we had with them all. Remember when you were brought the first hatchling, Imp? It was the most —"

He stopped when she looked at him, telling her how sorry he was for bringing it up. When no one asked her about it, she felt the need to tell them. It was the one reason she wished she'd not created the large creatures.

"The hatchling was beautiful. His wings had only just formed when his mother brought him to me. Even then, I thought him to be large, but he would, I know, have gotten so much larger. Ignis had already given him his flame, and he was getting used to it. Playing around in the forest with small balls of flames that he seemed to be enjoying. I'd been burnt a couple of times before I could set him on his feet to burn off some of the energy that newborn dragons have." Her heart broke when she thought of the next few minutes. "There were humans about—there always was one or two hiding for one reason or another. This group had…they'd been foraging for food. Mostly cave dwellers at that time. But they were atop the mountain behind us. They only wanted to frighten us away from the things that were in the valley. Fresh fruit. Some nuts thereabout. A smallish stone was tossed down the mountainside to have us afraid enough to move on. But it slid into something more, something no one could have predicted. Everyone started running away when it was obvious the landslide was growing by the minute. The little dragon was snatched up by his mother and moved. By the time the trees and the debris had finally made their final stop, the young hatchling and his mother had been crushed to death by one of the large boulders. It broke me in a way that I still hurt from to this day."

"Oh, how awful. The first child was killed.

I would have been so hurt by that as well." She told Carson she had been, but not as badly as Ava had been at the deaths. "She must have been a wonderful dragon. I'm assuming she was able to help the father with his loss."

"He died as well. Grief, it was simply too much for him. To have had it all and then snatched away killed him. At the time, and still to this day, it feels as if I had made a mistake in making the dragons for myself. I wanted to see their beauty. To marvel at their size. It had not occurred to me that anyone would want them dead. I know it was an accident, but the humans killed and killed until they nearly cleansed the earth of them." She looked around the room. "I'm sorry. I didn't mean to drag you into my pain. I will have Glacier tell you her part in the six sons of Coop being made into men."

"Could you have figured out a way for Coop not to have died?" Glacier told Cooper that she'd not been the one that had chosen what his payment would be. "I don't understand. He just died for no reason?"

"No. Nothing like that. But when he came to me, thinking I was a witch that could save his family, I asked him for a payment. It could have been anything he found of great value to himself. His riches, which even then your father had amassed a great deal of over the years after he was made. Coop could have told me he could have stayed away from the six of you, never coming into your life again. Anything he thought of as a value, he could have given me, and I would have been satisfied."

"He gave you his life?" Glacier nodded but looked so sad she wanted to tell Tristan, one of the sons, that he was being mean to her. "Can you explain to me how that went? I know my father wouldn't have just been able to live afar from us."

"No. That is what he told me that day too. He said that no matter the distance, he'd have to come back and make sure you were well. That you were able to make it in the human world. Coop even mentioned the gems and other riches he had but said he wouldn't need them as much as his sons would in starting out in the world of humans." Glacier smiled then. "Coop told me the only thing of value he had ever owned or wanted was in the six of you. He'd had it, he told me, with his mate too, but she had sacrificed herself already for their wellbeing. His words were that he could do no less than his mate had done in giving all that he was to them to make sure they were as safe as he could make them. From that day forward."

"He loved us." Glacier nodded, as did her and Ignis when Cooper spoke with so much emotion. "They loved us with everything they would ever have and made sure we could carry on, be able to move on in their image."

"It was more than that, I think. I think Coop knew the change was coming to a time that there would be no more dragons that only flew the sky. He was a smart dragon, as I have said, but he was smarter than most humans I've ever encountered." She pulled up the cave this time, the massive amount of riches that had been hoarded there. "As a dragon, he would have been able to save his tears and given those to you. And when he was created, there was a great many reasons for tears. The treasures here, some of them coins, gold, and other gems that he collected, were put aside for you. He'd even convinced his brother of the need to save for a rainy day. I don't know that he was able to tell what was coming. Magic was new to us all at that time. But I'd bet since it is something that a lot of dragons seem to have, his special magic was seeing parts of the future and what it might hold for all the dragons."

"It never occurred to me that the gems in there were larger than tears could have formed. Did he pick them up in his travels?" Imp told Cooper that he not only did that, but he was a whiz at bartering with other dragons. "What sort of thing would he need that wasn't there with him? I have to tell you this, Imp, I'm enjoying this more than I ever thought possible. I owe you a great deal for telling us this. Thank you. From the bottom of my heart."

"A merchant would come by once in a while. Coop would give me things that I'd trade for goods. It was amazing to me when I think of how trusting we were toward him. He was a funny man. I believe he was slightly off in his head, so you had to be careful not to cheat him. I think his mother would have been most upset with us had we done that. But Coop would have things like dragon scales. Broken up, of course, as they were as big as a person. Sometimes he'd have—oh, I nearly forgot. Once when the merchant came by, he had the most beautiful blooms with him. I don't know what they're called now, it has been so long, but he traded badly for them. And Coop gave them to his mate. Your mother wore them in a crown on her head until they were nothing but tatters."

When they finally left, after her exhausting herself, Imp made ready to return to her own place. It was George that stopped her, telling her that she could stay in the house and he'd go to her place. She was so touched by the gesture, with all the emotions that night, she kissed him on the cheek. The blast of power between them knocked them both apart, with her hitting the wall behind her hard enough that she was tossed from the house.

Chapter 4

George had worked at the computer for far too long when he was finally ready to call it quits. Instead of taking him only about an hour, he'd been sitting here for nearly five. His mind, he told himself, was just too bogged down with information.

It wasn't just information, he realized when he leaned back in his chair. It was also problems. Ones that he could see now that he'd not been able to before. Smiling, he thought of Imp when she'd awakened with him carrying her into the house after the kiss. That was what he was calling it now, the kiss. Like it had had all the magical beginnings of making love. It really didn't, but it was fun to tease Imp about it.

"What the hell are you doing toting me around like a child?" He told her he thought her being out in the yard wasn't very nice of him. "I'll know what I'm...what do you mean out in the yard? Never mind. I remember now. Stupid magic. Sometimes it just pisses me off when I'm not having a bad—what are you laughing about? I swear to you, George, you've been dropped on your head one too many times. Where are my brother and sister?"

"Ignas said he had magic to take care of. I didn't ask him what that meant. I figured that if he wanted me to know, he would have told me. Glacier was laughing hard when she disappeared. I think she might have hurt something. Or someone. I don't know." Imp glared at him harder. "You're very cute when you do that. Almost like you want me to kiss you again to see if this one will power me through the opposite wall."

"There won't be any more kissing between us." He wanted to tell her he thought she was wrong but didn't. He was sort of afraid she'd kill him. Winnie had told him that it really was within her power to kill all dragons with a snap of her fingers. Imp had looked so crestfallen that he wanted to comfort her in any way he could. "I'm going to hurt you, George. Or someone that you love."

"We just have to get used to each other, that's all. I'm sure I can come around to your way of thinking eventually. You're sort of mean, but I'm getting used to that. Falling in love with you isn't going to be hard either." She looked up at him at that moment, and he knew it had already happened. He was in love with her. Then he saw the tears. "Don't cry, love. I'm only kidding you about being mean. I mean, a little snappish, and you can put a person in their place with just a word, but I think you're under a great deal of stress right now."

"Your mother told me that you were too blunt for your own good. I can't say that I don't like it. At least I know where I stand at all times with you. And you me, if that's the way things are going to go." He nodded. "I'm afraid of everything. I'd only admit that to you, George, and I will kill you if you—"

"How about you try very hard not to tell me how much you want to kill me? I mean, I'm well aware that you can. It's been told to me no less than fifty times since we hit the walls. We'll just take that part off the table. If you'd not mind." She didn't look convinced it was a good idea, but she did concede that she'd try. "That's all I'm asking for."

That had been several hours ago. Almost as soon as they were getting ready to have breakfast—as they'd been out for that long before a faerie had found her under the wall and him under the car out front—George had tried to have a nice conversation with her. He did notice that she was easily distracted right now. However, he didn't think that was normal for her.

Hearing her coming down the hall, he was thrilled now that he'd waited to have lunch with her. As soon as she entered his office, he could smell heat. It was something he was used to, being around dragons all his life, but on her, it smelled like there was a bit of battle with it. He asked her if she was all right.

"I am. Now." He nodded, hoping she'd tell him more. "What is it you know about the people that live in the big house on the hill, some distance from here? The one that looks like it would have the most beautiful view of the town ever seen."

"Nothing. If you mean the Duggar Ranch, I only know it by name. We've been out there a couple of times to talk about selling off some of the cattle to the foundation so we could get much needed meat to other families. However, they never seem to be around where one of us can talk to them. Why do you ask?" She asked him another question. "Now that I can answer for you. But not for their operation, just in general. I have the information on my desk. Let me see. Two cows per five acres of land is what I was told. That's for cattle. I guess it would be different for different animals. As for corn, I can see what that says right now. Twenty-four pounds per day. This is what it says about the food. It's all dry matter. Grass hays will be about seven to ten percent moisture. It says here that you'd have to figure that ninety-two percent of their meal daily is dry, the rest will be the moisture. Why is that important?"

"A dragon can eat his body weight in food about three times a month. Then they can go for two to three weeks without anything other than water. Correct?" He said he wasn't positive about that, as he'd never been a dragon. "Can you ask your king idiot uncle about that?"

"Do I have to call him King Idiot?" George was laughing when he reached out to his uncle Cooper. After getting the correct answer for her, he asked what was going on. *I'm not sure yet. She's figuring. I'll let you know when I know. All right?*

Yes, but don't forget me. She'll make you. I don't think she respects me as a king. Do you? He told his uncle that he had no comment. *That's very telling, George. All right. Let me know if you need anything else. I need to repay her for helping at the bank too.*

This might be me, but I think I'd just let that go, Uncle Cooper. You're driving her nuts, bringing it up all the time. He said he owed her. *We all owe her if you want to be truthful about it. But I think pushing her into a corner will get your ass handed to you. In a big way.*

You might be right. I'll think on it. Uncle Cooper laughed. *Your aunt said the same thing. She said I was going to make her hurt me. Do you think she will?* All he said was *yes* before he broke the connection with him.

"According to records, there are approximately ten thousand acres that the Duggars have. When I was scouting around for a human that came up missing, I saw that there are less than a hundred cattle around the property. Might be a few more, but not enough to justify having that much land laying fallow." He wanted to point out to her that they didn't have to raise cattle there or a certain amount. Instead, he let her talk. "The land doesn't belong to the Duggars anymore, by the way. A corporation owns it now. The land was forfeited about ten years ago when they missed a balloon payment. I'm not entirely sure why they'd be still making balloon payments on land that has supposedly been in their family for generations, but I don't have that sort of pull to see the paperwork."

"I can call my mom for that sort of help. She and Aunt Carson work with some very well placed people. Let me give her a call." She asked if he could put it on speaker phone. "I can. Good idea. Then you can ask her what you want too."

After getting his mom on the phone, Aunt Carson joined them. As Imp told them what she was looking for, they set to work. In no time, not only did they have the reason for the balloon payment being missed, but also why they were still making them.

"The oldest son, his name is Elliot Duggar, had a gambling problem. I say had because he was killed not long after he put the land and all the cattle up for a bet. A sure thing turned out to be not so sure. That was about twelve years ago. The cattle were sold off to make half the payment back to the loan sharks that Elliot was working with, but since then, they've only been making about a quarter of the return. There isn't any money left for cattle, much less the feed to keep them. If you say it was bought up, I can see how legal that was as well. Elliot was in his forties when he was killed. I can't believe he could have been able to use the land in the first place, being that it wasn't in his name. Both his parents were alive then and running a successful cattle ranch. He did have a sister. I'll see if I can find her. Give me a few minutes here."

Mom spoke to them both while Aunt Carson did her research. "The house we're going to be moving into is nearly finished up. The faeries already started moving our things there last night. Xavier and I have been working with your brother Milo and Jamie in getting them more prepared for their new jobs." George told Imp that they'd become the Death Slayers for his parents. "What sort of magic did you get, George? I'm sure you have."

"I don't know yet. We've been getting to know one another." Imp huffed. "We're working on relationship skills right now. And not threatening to kill each other too. I think it's going swimmingly."

Mom laughed just as Aunt Carson said she had something. "The land was never in his name, just as I thought. There shouldn't have been any way he could have used it as collateral for a bet. I'm digging deeper here to find out the real deal. Something is fishy." Imp told Aunt Carson that she'd been all over the farm, and when she was finished looking, she had more information too. "All right. I guess you can get around as well as faeries can. Sometimes they're not sure what to look for when there is something amiss. Understand?"

"Not that they're jaded as I am, but they might think that seeing flowers is just fine. Hopefully, none of them have gone in there to help. It would mean certain death, I'm afraid. There is some underhanded fuckery going on there, Carson. Even from my height, I could see that they're not growing things for the cattle. I haven't any idea what would have to happen for someone go to in there and close that shit down, but it needs to happen before any more dragons or even kids get in there screwing around." Aunt Carson asked her if she was talking about marijuana. "That too, but opium poppies. Like acres and acres of it. Is that legal?"

"No. Not only is it not legal, but it's a federal crime. I'll get someone on it now. Do you think that the Duggars are doing it?" Imp told them she had no way of knowing who was in on it. "Never mind. I can see here that both the mister and missus are gone. As is the oldest son…holy Christ, she is the one that took the ranch from them. I can see it right here. Mother fuck. You're right, some underhanded fuckery is going on, and we'll get to the bottom of it. I'll see how to destroy the plants too."

When the connection was closed, his mom said she was proud of Imp. He could tell that Imp was embarrassed, but she thanked his mom. When he asked her what she wanted to do about dinner, she sat down across from him and didn't say anything for several minutes. He waited. One thing he'd learned in the last couple of days was that if Imp was rushed into anything, that was when she was at her worst.

"You might not have noticed this, but I'm not very social." He couldn't help it. George burst out laughing. When he saw her smile, he laughed again. "Right. So, I'd like to be. Honestly, I like being around your family. They sort of put up with me, and it's fun to get Uncle Idiot in a twist about shit. He does make it worth it to think up things to piss him off too easily."

"He was just talking to me about what he owes you." She growled. "I told him to just let it go. After telling him that I thought you'd hurt him, he said Aunt Carson said the same thing to him. I'm guessing, like you, he's doing this to get you pissy. Why would he do that? He knows you can hurt him."

"He's having fun, I guess. You do know that now I have to step up my game with him. While I'm more powerful than any of you, I'd never really hurt any of you. You are aware of that, aren't you?" George nodded and asked her to come to sit with him. "Sit with you where, you moron? You're sitting at a desk."

"Then sit on my desk or my lap." While he wasn't upset with her, she was sometimes too literal. "Come over here and let me hold you. I need that more than I need to breathe. Please? I just need to feel you close to me."

"No funny business." He didn't think having anything but business was going to be between them, but Imp did get up and come around to the business side of his desk. "You know what will happen if we were to have sex, don't you?"

"I'd be the happiest man on earth? I'd make you come so many times that you'd never want to leave the bed? You're going to have to narrow it down a little for me, love. My mind is in overdrive with that question." She told him he'd get more magic. "That is the least of my problems. I want to make you mine. I'm sure you figured that out by now. But more importantly, I want you to trust me. You don't. I mean, I don't think you do."

"I'm getting there." When she moved, he moved his chair back to accommodate her. When she faced him, her legs on either side of his hips, George felt his cock stretch and harden. "There is something you should know about me and having sex. I'm very loud."

"Christ, woman." He picked her up and put her on his desk amid her giggling. Looking up at her, his heart about as full as it had ever been, George told her what had been in his heart and mind for the last several days. "I love you, Imp. So very much. You have given me a reason to wake up in the morning. To smile. You've given me everything a man could ever hope to gain with a mate and so much more. Will you, someday, marry me? Be my wife?"

"I don't know. Can you afford me?" When

he tore her pants off, he could smell her arousal. "You've taken a very long time to get us to this point, George. Whatever will I do with you?"

"Love me." She looked like she needed to think about loving him, so he stood up. Dragging her mouth to his, he kissed her with all that he had. "Love me forever, Imp, and I'll make you the happiest woman ever born."

~*~

There was no time to tell him that she did indeed love him. Had since she'd figured out that he was about as matched to her as any person had ever been. Even her sister and brother didn't fit with her as much as George did. As soon as he laid her back on his desk, she knew she was in for something epic.

Wasting no time, he suckled her clit into his mouth until Imp screamed with the pleasure of it. Holding onto him seemed the only thing to keep her where she was. The need to get closer yet push him away to breathe was strong. But being enjoyed as she was made her eyes cross with pleasure.

His hands molded around her ass, massaging the large muscles. She cried out when he made her come when he bit down on her thigh. There wasn't any pain with his little bites. He made up for them with tiny kisses where he'd nipped her. Imp was working up to something amazing, something so profound that she thought perhaps it might be the end she'd been wanting. Holding on tighter to him, she begged him for more.

George ate her for what seemed like hours. Each time she thought she'd had more than enough, he'd touch her in a different spot, and she'd be begging once again. He fondled her breasts, pinched her hard, painfully full nipples. When he finally pulled from her pussy, all she could do was stare at him.

It wasn't just lust she saw in his face. There was pain too. She could understand both those feelings, having them herself. But it was the look of pure love that got her sitting up a little. Reaching out to touch his face, she was as much in love with George Manning as she had been with anyone or anything in her life. Running her finger down his cheek to his mouth, she felt her heart tighten up more when he kissed her finger.

"I love you, George. I didn't think I'd ever find love, much less someone in my life that makes me feel so special. And you do. Right now, I'd give you the world." He said she'd given him enough with her love. "I so very much love you."

He didn't take his eyes off hers as he fisted his cock. She could feel the movement of his hand as he leaned closer to her. When he was right at her entrance, he paused, like he was waiting for her permission. Giving it to him, giving him everything, she cried out loud enough that she heard glass shatter somewhere in the room. The chandelier above them shook with it as he entered her.

Imp looked around from where she was. George was still inside of her, and she adjusted her legs to wrap around him. When he groaned, she finally looked at him. He was smiling at her, but no less painful than before.

"I thought you weren't going to come back to me." She asked him if she'd passed out. "You certainly did. And so you know, I'd like to tell the world that I made my mate faint, but just knowing I did that will bring me such a happy smile."

"You're sappy." He moved then, his big body taking her to such heights. "Oh yes, George. Make me come again and again. I need it so badly. Make me yours."

"Yes, ma'am."

He took her gently at first, his hands moving

over her body again and again. His mouth took her breast. His cock made her scream over and over, while his hands made short work of her muscles tightening up. And when he took her mouth again, this time almost savagely, Imp came hard enough that she bit him. The taste of blood filled her mouth, and then she was out again.

When she woke this time, she was in the big bed she'd been sleeping in. The other side of the bed was warm, so she sat up to stretch and find George. He was in the bathroom talking on the phone. Handing her the notes he'd been taking, he kissed her on the mouth and told Carson he was putting her on speaker phone.

"Imp is here with me. You don't have to start from the beginning, but can you tell her what you've been able to find out? Then I'll fill in the rest." She said she didn't mind. This was a huge help to everyone. "Good. It's not just about helping people get their feet back under them, but taking them out from under them when they screw up."

Carson brought her up to date on things. "Yes, it is. Doris Duggar is dead, thankfully. Last night there was a raid on the property that ended in the death of five men she had working for her.

Even if it wasn't for the opium she was producing, she still would have ended up arrested had she not gotten killed when her men turned on her. There were so many drugs in the place that I think we could have supplied the entire world with them. And the men she had working for her were chained to their tables like animals. Pissing in bottles so she could meet production." Imp asked what would happen now. "I have to have the big guys go in and take care that there isn't anyone waiting to just step into her shoes. I don't think she would have lasted long in prison. One of the places she worked for would have gotten to her. Or she might well have kept right on producing the shit."

"I can take care of the poppies if you want. I can go in and use a little magic and kill off the roots. Then I'll go in and destroy the heads of the flowers." George asked her why that was important. "If we just kill off the plants, the heads could very well resow themselves. That won't be helpful to anyone. I'll have to think of a way to gather them or destroy them that is safe for everyone. That way, there won't have to be any more damage to the earth."

"Dragon's breath would harm the earth,

right?" She looked at George, thinking about what he was saying. "I could call one of my brothers to come and help with that part. I mean, if one of them were to put a hot breath over the dead poppies, it should destroy the seeds inside, right?"

"I think that might work." She looked out the window to think. Imp loved that the bathroom in this room had a large window that showed the back yard. Instead of seeing tile like most did, this view afforded a person time to think and to relax while bathing. "It would have to be done before the rains come in. I'd hate to think that once the roots are all dead, the seeds might have time to regerminate."

"Rachel." She looked at George. "She can throw these balls of flame at things, and while it burns hot, it doesn't linger. I can ask her to come help. She'd be thrilled to know her magic can do something helpful like that."

"You ask her, and I'll go get her. Once I get the roots killed off, I can make sure she gets the rest." Imp kissed George on the mouth before winking at him. "I knew you'd be good for something other than the best sex I've ever had."

His face turned a bright red when Carson laughed. It was a hardy laugh, too, like she'd been as caught off guard as George had been. Imp didn't say she was sorry — it was enjoyable to see him flustered and to hear such good laughter. When the phone was closed, she stepped into the shower to get cleaned up. Imp heard George on the phone.

"All right," he told her after stepping in the shower with her. Taking the sponge that she'd been using, he filled her in on what Rachel said as he scrubbed her back. "Finn is going to meet us there. He said he doesn't want to leave any of us alone when there could be trouble from some of the other people involved. I agree. There is no telling who or what might happen over the next few days."

She washed her hair, then his back. This was the first time she could remember that she lingered in the shower. Usually, she was in and out before her hair was fully rinsed. When they were finished up, Imp handed him a towel when she had wrapped up in one of her own.

"Can you tell if I got any magic from you?" She asked him to put out his hand. When she touched the back of it, great long claws spread out from his fingertips. "Well, that's disturbing. Why would I have something like that? Or do you know?"

"The only reason I know is when we were making love, you cut me a few times. It heals right away, but it was startling the first time." He told her how sorry he was. "There is no need for that. I sort of enjoyed it. As for what else you might have, I think you have the same powers I do. I want you to look in the mirror and tell me what you see. I see it, but I'm not sure anyone else can."

He did as she asked, the towel hanging precariously over his hips. It took him several moments to find what she'd been talking about. When he did, he turned to her and looked into her eyes.

"I didn't notice that before on you." She told him he wasn't supposed to. "I guess I can understand that. It would be hard to blend in with humans if your eyes sparkled like they do. Christ, Imp, you're stunning. There are stars and planets in the colors of your eyes. The longer I look, the more I see."

"I see in yours what I've never seen in my own." They stared at one another for some time before she pulled away. "There are other things you got. I'm not sure if it was a combination of the two of our magic or something else. You can heat the earth. Also, freeze it. I can as well, but I have to work at the heat. I can ignite Ignis or freeze people, one or two at a time, but you have the same ability as my brother and sister."

"Is that bad?" She turned then, looking him in the face. "You think it's bad, don't you? I can't think of a single thing right now other than I believe I've disappointed you."

"Why on earth would you think that?" George told her she looked upset. "I'm not upset *at* you, but for you. George, your heat right now will surpass your idiot uncle. Not only that, but with the power you have now, you could easily end him."

"I'd never do that." Imp told him she didn't think he would, but "the idiot" might be pissed about it. "Are you going to call him the idiot for the rest of your life? I love it, but I'm thinking he might take you to task about it if you keep it up."

"When he stops bothering me about the payment to me, then I'll call him by his name. Not until then. He opened this door when I told him I didn't want anything." She smiled at George. "I can't hurt him—well, I could, but I won't. I need to have fun too. And I am. I don't know that I've had this much fun in…well ever."

They were sitting out on the front steps when Finn and Rachel arrived. She looked a little flustered, but a quick check of her mind had her nearly bursting out laughing. Rachel was terrified of her. There really wasn't a good reason for it, but she was. As soon as she bounced them, what she called teleporting to the area, it looked as if her magic was about done with killing off the plants.

"My goodness. There is so much of it, isn't there?" She nodded and wasn't surprised that Finn was brought by George. He did it well, too and didn't seem to have told his brother it was his first time. She was still laughing when Rachel and Finn began laying a layer of heat, enough to kill the seeds. Imp thought she might have to take things down a little if she wanted to hang out with this family other than a working environment. She was beginning to have fun and wanted to keep it up.

Chapter 5

Glacier watched the ice and snow as it slid down the mountainside. She was doing maintenance on the mountain tops for Dawn today. It was something she knew had to be done, and usually, it was relaxing. Not today, however. It worried Glacier that there was so much coming down when she felt someone new touching her mind. She smiled when she figured out it was George.

Hello. She told him hello back. *I have two questions for you. They're just... I don't know, as in I don't know how to phrase the question in a way so you'd understand what I'm asking you. Not that I don't think you're brilliant. You are. So much more than I am. I think I'm mucking this up.*

No. Go ahead and ask me. I'd love to be able to help you with anything you need. He explained what had happened. Glacier sat down hard. *You mean you're* almost *as strong as I am, right? And that your heat is* almost *as strong as my brother's. You meant that, didn't you? Please say you meant that.*

I didn't. And I didn't mean to scare you. I can feel it. Like we're sharing it. I'm not sure what I said to frighten you, Glacier, but I'm very sorry for it. She told him they would share their feelings if he was able to match her magic, completely ignoring where her thoughts had gone in the first place. *Good to know that too. Let me write that down. Okay. Back to the other part. What I'm wondering is if you can come and help me be better at my craft. Ice is trickier than fire, I've come to figure out. Or better yet, I guess, would be for me to come to you. That way, there isn't any trouble at this end for Imp and my family.*

Does Imp know about this? Not you getting help — she'd praise you for seeking out someone that could help you — but that your heat and ice are so powerful? George told her that was how he'd found out. She'd told him. *I see. Well, I don't, but that's all right too. Yes, you can come to me. If you feel my emotions, then you'd be able to pinpoint where I am.*

He was suddenly in front of her. Hugging him to her for no other reason than she could, Glacier showed him what she'd been doing. How taking some of the stress off the mountain would help the villages below, as well as the animals grazing. Making the grass grow faster. When she realized that she was babbling, she closed her mouth before starting again.

"Dawn usually does it, but she's been working on keeping things going on her end on a new area. You should go and see it. It's a lovely garden that will have people coming around for decades. I've been there—" George said her name. "I'm nervous. Very much so, as a matter of fact. But it's fine. It's not you, but—I was worried that I might flood the area below too much."

Glacier was worried about that, so it wasn't a lie. However, that wasn't what was forefront in her mind. George was. Her sister too, but George seemed to not understand the implications of what was actually going on right now.

"I would guess it has to be a perfect balance." She nodded and asked him, changing the subject, what he'd been able to figure out on his own. "Mostly not to freeze up things that are living. I've not killed anything. Yet. But I've come close to hitting the stray cat that lives — well, he used to live in the barn — with one of my balls of ice. I know I don't have to make them into balls — I do the fire that way too, so it's just easier for me to have something physical when I'm playing around. Now I'm babbling." He smiled at her, and she couldn't help but smile back at him. "I don't want to take up your time if you're busy. I can learn this at another time."

Glacier assured him that now was a perfect time. As they worked through his methods, mostly how to aim and such, she finally convinced him to do things an easier way, just to try it a couple of times. Standing behind him, she showed him what to look at. How to shove the magic at the object.

"This will work because you're not showing whoever what you have in the way of a ball of ice, but just let it flow from your fingertips. Remember what I said about your knob that you turn up for the temperature? Well, you don't have to necessarily freeze things solid so much as just sort of put it out of commission for a while. Like this." Aiming her magic at the stone on the bottom of the little creek by where she was living, the little stone leapt from the water and froze the waterway around it for a few inches. "It will warm up in the water, and then it'll be fine. And I did ask the stone first if you could practice on him. That's important to remember, George. That everything has a life within it. Even a dead tree will have things feeding off it, as well as perhaps living there. The stone said he'd do anything for the king's nephew. He also is afraid of your mate. I don't know, but I'd say he's right in that."

"Imp?" She nodded at George when he laughed. "I was surprised by that. I mean, she's powerful in her own right. Imp told me that she was going to have to calm her jets a little. I had no idea what that meant at first. I was thinking she was powered around by jet propulsion or something. Getting to know each other is sort of scary at first, but I love her with all my heart. Anyway, she is going to try not to be so literal when she listens to people. That part, she said, would take a while to get down."

They worked for over five hours on his magic. Imp spoke to her three times while he was there with her. None of it was very important. Glacier thought she was just making sure George was all right. The first time she wanted to make sure he'd made it. Then she told her about how he'd popped Finn into where they were working.

I can imagine that went over well. Imp said he'd not told his brother yet that it had been his first time. *Oh, Imp, that's going to be epic when he does. I'm sure he's going to be none too happy with his brother. Then terrified when he starts thinking about the things that could have gone wrong. Oh, how I wish I could be there when or if he ever does.*

Yes, well, the thing is, he's doing a great job with all this. And so patient with me as I get to know him. I can be cranky sometimes. Prudently, she didn't comment to her sister. Who, she thought, was more than cranky all the time. *And he's showing me how he keeps track of things for the Manning Foundation on this end of the United States. They have been taking care of the underdog for as long as they've been changed to shifters.*

Now that I'm aware of them, I notice the things around the world when I go places that I work. Why, just this morning, I saw a shipment of bottled water coming in on a flight that I was over. You know how I like to make sure there is no trouble on a plane, so I scan it? No name on the donations, of course, but I could see them on it. Imp said she was enjoying just watching them get things prepared to go out. *I bet they'll be doing this for the rest of their days too.*

Helping without anyone knowing who or where the help came from.

Working with George made her feel like she was getting to see her sister and brother. Ignis was hard to get to pop in and see, but Imp was nearly impossible to visit. She was forever going from one place to the next, trying to make some money. Or simply hanging out with humans. Imp seemed to enjoy their company, but at the same time, she didn't care for them. It was an odd thing. But then so were some of the things Glacier did.

When George left her, she sat down near the creek they'd been working around to think. He had caught on quickly, and she was impressed. Glacier supposed that being around other creatures all his life, he would know control better than most. Almost as soon as she thought of what had entered her mind earlier, Ignis contacted her.

I just heard from George. She told him how he'd just left her. *I'm going to help him. That'll be fun to get to know him. But he said he's as powerful as I am. And you know what, Glacier? He fucking is. Maybe a little more so. What the fuck is going on? Is he going to be replacing us?*

Why would that be the first thing that popped into your head? Don't think like that, or you'll stress yourself out. You're as bad as Imp sometimes. But I've been thinking about him all afternoon while we were working. Ignis, he's powerful like us both. Do you have any idea what that means? He said he'd just told her that. *Damn it. Listen to what I'm saying. George is as powerful as both of us, and he's with Imp.*

You're saying something, but I'm not getting it. Just tell me what has you all worked up, and I'll tell you you're wrong and — When he stopped making fun of her, she waited. She felt the exact moment that he understood what she was saying to him. *Glacier. He. Is. With. Imp. The world is still here. So are we. Even if he'd only been with you, there could have been a chance that one of you might well have been hurt. Did you touch him? I mean, have physical contact with him, Glacier?*

I made sure I did. Several times. Hugging him, I have to tell you, is the best thing ever. As close as I've been to anyone lately, and I soaked it up while I was with him. Ignis was laughing so hard she just knew he was dancing around his cave. *This might not come to anything, but I would give anything to be able to hug you and Imp again. I know that you and I can be together a little bit, but not with Imp at all. What do you think the chances are that we'll be able to hug? All the time?*

I don't know. But I'm right there with you. The last time we were all together was when she was creating dragons. Glacier thought about that day now and wondered how they'd ever survived it. Even with the help of Imp.

The blast was so…I think you're right in thinking we shouldn't have survived it. It took down that entire mountain in one second. The creatures around there never had time to move, get out of the way of the heated stones and ice. As it was, Imp was badly hurt, as were you. I still, to this day, haven't any idea how I ended up not having any broken body parts.

Imp threw you clear. She did me as well when she got to me. The landing so far away is what hurt me. Don't you remember that? Ignis said he didn't remember much other than they'd parted that night, never to be a trio again. *That hurts my heart so much, too, Ignis. There are times over the years that I just wanted to come see the two of you and damn what might well happen. We couldn't even help our sister with her pain when she was hurt that day. Or, for that matter, any other day before either.*

To be honest with you, Glacier, it's the reason I don't interact with humans. I did, for a long time, but when I'd see something I'd want to show the two of you, it broke me to not be able to tell you about it.

My discovery when I started to make the furniture was something I so desperately wanted to share, but I couldn't be near enough for you to touch it. I would see yours or Imp's faces on the humans I was around. It was just too much for me. She felt his pain, so much like her own that she often wondered why the world was able to go on turning when they had been hurt so badly. *We did so much for the world. Everything we did, it was with the mindset that it was to improve things for every living thing. Then, in one hug, that was all it took for us to be tossed away like we were no longer useful to the world. That our magic was no longer helpful, so they separated us forever.*

They both cried then. Not close, as they both needed at that moment, but far away. She was just getting ready to flee to her home, to hide out in there, when George appeared in front of her. And he had Ignis with him.

"I felt your pain." She nodded at George when he spoke softly, never taking her eyes off her brother. "I never...it never occurred to me that we could all be together. I have an idea that it needs to be the four of us. A balance, as you said. The two of you with Imp and myself will be the best for all of us, don't you think? I know she misses you. Everyday. I see the longing in her face when she thinks of you. I think, and I'm just hoping here, that we can take care of this forever."

He grabbed them both, pulling them in for a tight hug. The tingle of something had her nearly pulling away, but he held her steadfast. It was Ignis that wrapped his arms around her first. Then she did the same to him and George. It was, she thought, the second most wonderful feeling in the world. Now she just needed her sister in the group.

Pulling away from the two of them, she saw the tears on their cheeks and wiped at her own. Watching as a beautifully shaped emerald slid from George's eyes, she touched it with her finger, and it appeared on a chain around her wrist.

"Oh, George. Look at this. It's beautiful. But I can't accept this. It's for love." He told her that he did love her. Ignis showed her that he had one as well. "You love us both?"

"Of course I do. My goodness, woman, you're my sister. Ignis is my brother. And by my heart too. Yes, I couldn't love you two any more than if you were related by blood." He touched the emerald, and she saw a heart form in the middle of it. George frowned. "I didn't know I could do that, but isn't that nice?"

They hugged again, this time talking over each other as they talked about how wonderful it was. How good it felt to be together. George hugged them to him again, and she knew as soon as she pulled back that they were no longer at her place but the home that George shared with her sister.

"We should go back. What if we're wrong about this? This could be disastrous for everyone." She turned when she heard something break. Her sister stood there, her mouth open and wide-eyed. At her feet, spreading out around her, was liquid, along with broken glass. She thought it was sweet tea.

"Hello, Imp. Come give me a hug."

~*~

Imp wasn't sure what she was to do now. Having her family there, all three of them, in not just the same county but the same house, was boggling her mind. Getting up again to hug them, she heard her sister laugh.

"I just want to get as much as I can in the event something goes wrong." Glacier said she didn't think it would. That having them together then taking them apart would be beyond cruel. "I agree, but when have things ever gone our way in matters of magic?"

"The dragons. Which I'm eternally grateful you created." George hugged, then kissed her. "I have a couple of things I'm working on for the foundation, but I wondered if you guys can answer some questions. The place that has asked for money to improve — that's all they said was to *improve* — I believe you might know, Ignis. It's the hardware store near where I picked you up. I don't know if you make your tools or buy them, but this man, Benson is his last name, says he's run into some terrible weather there and that he's going to have to close up or improve. The weather, has it been any different than it has been for years?"

"Are you asking me if I messed with the weather, young man?" They both laughed, and it took her a moment to realize that Ignis had made a joke. She didn't think she'd ever heard him do that before. "No, I'm not in the habit of — are you talking about that old man that runs off kids when they come by? He's an old bastard, and I'd not buy from or lend him a single thing. What is the amount he wants? Did he at least give you what he'd like to improve with?"

"Five hundred thousand. He's saying there is room for improvement around town with other buildings he owns. The thing is, I can't even find a hardware store under his name. There is one owned by a Mark Fire, but nothing more." Imp understood it a second before George did. "You own the building the hardware store is in."

"I do own the building, but not the hardware store. And in order for him to make any kinds of improvements, he'd have to get it cleared by me." George told him that was a smart move on his part. "I have been around the block a couple of times. Is there any way you can get more information? As you can well imagine, I have no use for a kiln to dry my wood. And I don't see that anyone in town would either. That's the only real expense I can see him using that sort of money for. I mean, there just isn't much in the way of building going on there anyway. Not so that your regular homeowner would do it. Do you mind asking?"

"Not at all. I'm glad for the input from you."

When the two of them went out of the room, Imp and Glacier sat down on the couch. Glacier stared out the open doorway where the men had gone.

"I don't want to let either of you out of my sight for the same fear you have. I don't know what I'd do if this was all taken away from me again." She finally sat down next to her and took her hand into hers. "I have a favor to ask of you. I'd like to go shopping. Out to lunch with you. I see people doing that all the time, and I've always thought it would be so much fun for us to do that. Even your mother-in-law would be fun, I think."

"Sure. It's almost noon now. How about I reach out to Cindi and see if she has time?" She said that would be perfect. "If the others are around still, would you like to be with them too? It's entirely up to you. I'm really good at telling people no."

"You make that sound like you've only just realized you can do that. Imp, you've been doing that our entire lives." Glacier was in such a good mood. She usually was, but it was so nice to hear her laughing in person. Also, she'd simply missed hanging out with her. "Yes, I'd like for you to invite them all if they'll come. It'll be wonderful to be able to talk like this is an everyday occurrence."

Imp was not only able to get the women gathered up, but she talked George's brothers into taking out George and Ignis. Like her sister, she didn't want to let this end. She knew she would be begging Cooper to end her life if someone were to snatch this away from her.

"All right. We'll meet them there. They too can just pop in and out, so that's what I thought you and I would do so we can do some shopping as well. There are a couple of things I would like to get for the new baby that one of the pack members is going to have. Did you know that Rachel is the daughter of the alpha? I just found out." Glacier said she'd like that as well.

The two of them entered the office where Ignis and George were, and they were having a good time. After telling them what they were doing and that one of George's brothers was going to contact him soon, they started out the door, only to be called back.

"I need a hug in the worst kind of way." She smiled at George. He'd been saying he was slightly jealous about all the hugs going on. When she wrapped her arms around him, loving the way his body molded to hers for the best kind of hug, Glacier and Ignis joined them. Group hugs were the very best.

Just as she was finishing that thought, something started to happen to them. There was no time to separate. The magic poured over the four of them quickly. Imp knew the others were experiencing the same thing, as their faces were registering shock. She wasn't going to allow this to happen. No one or nothing was going to separate them again. But there was nothing she could do.

When the magic seemed to cover them from the top of their heads to their feet, they were dragged back, still touching, to form a circle with their hands together. Being bent backwards, to the point where she could see the ceiling, didn't hurt, but she could no longer see the others. She could tell they were in the same position, each of them still holding on and looking at the ceiling in the office.

There wasn't any way she could escape from this. Her tears filled her eyes when she thought of the fun she was going to miss with her family. Just as suddenly as she thought that, a light, as bright as the sun, came through the ceiling above them. It hit the circle that the four of them had made when they were clinging to each other. Imp closed her eyes, telling her family the best she could how much she loved them.

When she woke up, not even sure when she'd fallen back, she looked around for everyone. They were laying on the floor with her. George had a bloody nose, and it looked like Ignis had hurt his hand. He and George had been the closest to the desk, so she assumed they'd hit it when they fell. Crawling to George, she woke him up when he didn't move quickly enough for her.

"Are you all right?" He just stared at her. With a smack to his cheek, she asked him again. "If you don't answer me, damn it, I'm going to hurt you."

"You already did." He sat up and pulled her into his arms. "Christ, what the hell was that? I feel like I've been run over a couple of times. Holy Christ. Did you get that information too? It hurt when it was being downloaded into my head, but it processed quickly. What's wrong?"

She could only stare at him as he sat there smiling at her. Imp asked him if he was having a stroke or something. His laughter caught her off guard.

"No, I'm not having a stroke. I'm just so happy to see that you're all right, as well as Ignis and Glacier." Ignis and Glacier sat up then, and she asked them the same thing. They at least answered her. "But, back to my question—did you get the information that seemed to be planted in my head?"

"The dragon eggs." She looked at Ignis when George nodded. "Yes, I got that. They're…

do you really think they're in the big barn? I knew you had a big barn, but for some reason, I don't think that's the one they're in."

"What the fuck are you talking about?" Glacier laughed, and she wanted to smack her too. "What information? What dragon eggs? The three of you are pissing me off. Didn't any of you feel that shit that went down? That fucking hurt, you know. What is wrong with you guys?"

As soon as she said the words, she had to hold her head still while the information seemed to do just what George had said—it was downloaded into her brain. Not only that, but she knew it *was* a different barn than the one they had now. Also, there was some information about gems left behind. While she did understand what that might mean, she was confused about a great many things right now. However, things were coming clearer more and more.

"I want to see."

When Glacier helped her up, she went with her to the back door. There were so many faeries at the doorway that she thought something had happened. Asking them if they wanted to go inside to be safe, they just stared out beyond the house.

"Is no one going to answer my questions to —? Holy fuck." The barn, a very generic term for what looked like a plane hangar, stood next to the barn that was there when George bought the house. Imp didn't know why, but she was reasonably sure it was going to be larger once a person was inside of it. "If that is filled with eggs and someone expects me to nurse them, you're fucking out of your mind. What the hell are we supposed to do with them if that sucker is filled to the brim?"

"You brought them here. The four of you." No one moved when Cooper stood in front of them. Since he didn't appear there in the last few minutes, she thought the magic or whatever the hell it was had brought him too. "They're not for you to nurse — however, the thought of that makes me giggle. These are for the dragons that might well have lost their loved ones long ago. A mate or a child that they no longer have. Some of the eggs have no family left, a great many of them, as a matter of fact. But since the magic brought them here to you and your family, I would imagine you four are going to make sure they get to a good place to bring them to life. Would you mind taking a look with me? Since I was summoned here, I'd like to have a look around."

"Wait. Wait. There's more." Imp looked at the other three. She could really hate the lot of them right now. She thought their sappy smiles were a ploy to make her pissed off more. "There are gems too. Left behind by dragons that were storing them for their family and have been abandoned. I have a feeling there is a great deal more of that than there are dragon eggs. Why the hell would they just leave it hidden and not tell anyone?"

"I would think so they'd be able to go back to it when it was needed. As for not telling anyone, I'm sure they might well have. But they, too, have gone away. It's sad, don't you think, to know they worked hard, and it would have been for them to have stored such valuables away for trading. As you told us the other day, my dad traded things for gems and other things. Do you suppose he told them to do that?" Imp told Cooper she was sorry she'd been so cruel about saying that. "You did nothing wrong, Imp. You're right. But it is sad too. However, the gems and the money we can get from them will go to helping dragons get to a place where they can be safe from humans. Especially the hatchlings. We'll buy up as much land as we can with it and set it up for them. This is going to bring dragons back. I know people will be terrified of them being there. But perhaps we can keep them as safe as my father did. By making us shifters to blend in with them."

"I can do that." Imp asked her sister what it would cost the dragons that needed it. "I'll know that when they tell me. I have a feeling that whatever the cost, it will never be as great as the one your father paid, Cooper. I have said this before, and I will forever say it. Your mother and father were the greatest dragons and parents ever made."

"Thank you for that. You've no idea, or perhaps you do, how wonderful it's been having the three of you here to tell us stories about them." They made their way to the barn and opened the big door. She could see the sparkle of gems as the sun touched the areas. Before they were only a few feet into the large opening, the other Mannings joined them. Sons of Coop, first born children, Coop's grandchildren, as well as the other brothers to George. "Well, my family. Are we ready to see what we have here?"

Skipping lunch had been something she normally didn't like to do. But magically making her some celery and carrots to eat made her feel better. Imp shared them with anyone that wanted any. It staved off the hunger pangs for them all, she thought.

There were, as far as they could see, over five hundred unhatched eggs. There were so many colors and designs on them that she hadn't any idea how they came to be. It wasn't until Carson came to talk to her that she realized how she'd done this for all the dragons.

"Dragons didn't mate with their own color, I'm guessing." Imp told Carson that it never occurred to her to make that stipulation. "I'm glad you didn't. It's going to be an amazing thing to see these eggs paired with a dragon and see what becomes of it. How do you know if they're still viable? I mean, it's been centuries they've been evacuated, right?"

"There are a few that are newly made. Not that many, however. But in answer to your question, yes, I can tell. As you would be able to as well should you put your hand on one of them." Imp pointed to the one that was in front of them. "Touch your hand to that blue one there. And so you know, it's sapphire. The diamonds in the shell seem to have come from a dragon much like your sons."

Imp knew her pain when Carson realized that the unborn dragon was no more. Dead was the word that humans used, but she hated it. "No more" seemed to say it all without the four letter word that hurt so many people.

"What will you do with it?" Carson stepped back and looked at her when she didn't answer. "It's so beautiful. I hate to think that—"

"Touch it again, queen of dragons." Carson didn't move for a couple of seconds, then put her hand on the egg. "As you can tell, he's alive now. You, with your power and pain, gave him the chance that he needed. Should you, and only you, touch the other eggs that are no more, then you will bring them back. I haven't any idea why I know that, but it worked, so that's a great beginning for them. Don't you think?"

There were fifty such eggs that had been empty of life when she'd gone around the cavernous room. But with Carson's magic, all but four were now ready to be given to a dragon. The ones she wasn't able to bring back had had damage done to the shell. Imp thought that perhaps they'd be able to break down the gems on them and use that. However, she didn't want to do that to something so beautiful unless it was needed. They were, simply put, the most beautiful things she'd ever created.

Chapter 6

It took them almost three days to get the eggs cataloged and a nice list of what kind they were. Then, just when they thought they had it down, it was Imp that discovered they were getting more in daily. Not as many as the first time, just one or two at a time, but it was overwhelming to think of how many dragons had left behind their children for one reason or another.

"They were killed. You get that, right? Dragons would never leave their hatchlings unless they were killed or murdered to prevent them from keeping them safe." George told Ignis that he didn't want to think of so many deaths. "I can understand that. I do. I want to ask you something while we're on the talk about what might have happened with the dragons. Do you suppose their bones are someplace? Or do you think they've been picked over so much that there isn't a trace of them left?"

"Why would that be important? Not that I don't think you might have a point, I just don't know what we'd be able to do about it." Ignis told him. "Okay. I guess I can see that. Bones being found would have humans asking a lot of questions we don't want to answer. Did you ever find any when you were living in the caves?"

"Yes. A great many of them. The deeper in the caves I explored when I was living off the grid, they call it, the more complete the dragon's skeleton would be. I usually had the faeries gather up whatever I found and take them to the gardens they'd create." George asked him if there had been any information he could glean from the bones. "You mean like a clan or whatever? No. I mean, I could see how they lost their lives. I also found a great many warrior fae that had died with them."

"Warrior fae? I think I've heard of them. My uncle, he told us that a fae would be paired with a dragon when they were small, and they'd train together. After they were deemed a working pair, they'd be pressed into service to care for places that could afford a dragon and his leader." Ignis said he had it right. However, most of the time, they were never cared for well. "I don't know how that would work when someone is waiting on payment and riding a big fucking dragon."

They both laughed, coming up with ways the dragon and fae would get back at the person that was past due on bills. When it was apparent that they weren't going to get anything done for being silly, the two of them went out into the sunshine. The sun, after being inside so much over the last few days, felt good.

"I've enjoyed hanging out with you, George. You're a good man. If I had to pick someone to be mated to my sister, it would have been you. Hands down, you're the best." George thanked him without opening his eyes to see the other man. "George, are you napping right now?"

"No. Just enjoying nature for a few minutes. Did I tell you that the gems and other things that were brought to us have been sorted as well? Most of them are rubies, which I guess I can understand. Anger must have been something dragons would feel for a long time." Ignis didn't say anything. He turned to see what had silenced the man and looked to where he was staring. "Please tell me you're seeing this as well. I mean, I don't know if we should run, but it's the most beautiful site I've seen in a while."

"It's real. They're fae, George. A great many of them too." Watching as the swarm came at them, he was nearly ready to go back into the barn when one of the many landed on the ground in front of him, bowing before the two of them. "George, contact your uncle. He might be able to feel them, but I'd make sure if I were you."

"Are we in trouble?" Ignis said he didn't know what was going on. He told his uncle what was going on and who was with him. "Uncle Cooper is coming. He said he felt them too. Why is she not moving?"

"You need to tell her that she can." Ignis nodded when he looked over at him. "She's bowing before you, not me. For some reason, I don't know yet, she's pledging herself to you."

"My uncle is coming. He's the king of dragons." The woman glanced up at him but stayed where she was. She told him she wasn't a dragon. "I know that. I mean, I can see that. However, I— Do you suppose you could stand up and talk to me? You're making me very nervous right now."

She stood up, and he could see that she was not just beautiful but armed as well. There was a sword at her side that seemed to sing to him. Right now, with her hand on the pummel, he wasn't nervous but somehow knew she stood that way all the time. At the ready, he thought.

Her face had a few scars on it. Nothing that distracted from her beauty, but he would imagine they'd been quite painful when she'd been hurt. The tight fitting clothing she had on told him she was built for war. That she wouldn't have had to work very hard to have maintained her muscles.

"I'm Helenia, leader and trainer of the fae riders." He put out his hand, and she seemed not to understand what he was doing. "I have been sent here to help you with the hatchlings. I am aware of them being stored here when they arrive. The others with me, all fae riders, are willing to do whatever you need to help."

"I don't know what I'm doing right now. I mean, we just made a list of what there is in there. Who sent you?" She said the world felt the movement of so many dragons. "Dawn, the mother of the earth, she sent you then?"

"Dawn? Mother Earth?" George told her that was her. "I know no one by that name. As I said, the world sent me to help with the care of so many dragons. The earth and all her rulers. The ones that care for the water, air and anything else that makes this world what it is All the lords and ladies that care for each part that makes the whole of the earth. All of the different rulers of the world have a good stake in what you're doing and have pledged to help in any way possible."

"George? Who is this?" He explained to his uncle who the woman was. When he was finished, George was no closer to figuring out who had sent her than before. He said so to his uncle. "Ah, that I can help you with. As she said, all the elements have a ruler. While I rule the dragons, there are many more rulers of the dragons that are beneath me. They are the ones that follow the rules that I set forth. Also, they'll send help, should I approve it, when there is a great need. I'm assuming that since you said the world was going to benefit from the hatchlings, everyone wants to have their name in the hat when you decide where the dragons will be raised."

"Me?" George knew his voice squeaked when he spoke but didn't care. "You're the king of dragons. Where would I fit into that scenario for where they go?"

"They're not yet dragons, now are they?" George was still thinking on that when Helenia cleared her throat. He was grateful to Uncle Cooper for him getting more information. His mind was still on the fact that he was going to be in charge of the eggs. With Imp, of course, but still…. "How many fae have you brought to George here, Lady Helenia? It looks like a great deal."

"I have brought all that could follow. Some are fae, yes, my lord, but there are a great many other creatures as well. Brownies, as well as faeries that were at one time in service for the dragons. As well as quite a few under creatures, such as the ones that take care of the earth they'll be stepping upon. Even the waterways are here, awaiting the word from Lord George to start breeding more fish and other sea creatures to feed those that care for the little ones." Helenia bowed low and stood again with a smile upon her face. "There were so many that wanted to come only to see the hatchlings that are gathered. It was something, I must say, to have them disappear from their resting spots. And the gems we all were piling too. To see them disappear, only to hear that they were with the great hope for all the little ones left behind."

"Helenia?" George had seen Imp coming toward them, but when she stopped suddenly and called out the other woman's name, he could see the joy on each of their faces as they hugged. "I thought you no more all these years. I'd given up on finding you. Where have you been hiding?"

"Nay, not hiding, my lady. I've been resting all these years. It took the earth to wake me after the explosion of that day. I was hurt that badly. It is said that you saved a great many of the fae and other creatures. I thank you for that." Imp, as he knew she would, waved off the thanks. "Are you here to help with the hatchlings? 'Tis going to be a great sight to see them in the skies again, don't you think?"

"I do. But I'm the mate to George. My brother and sister are here as well." They both looked at Ignis, who seemed to be tongue-tied. However, he wasn't looking at the fae but the field beyond. "Ignis? What is it? Do you see something we don't?

"Plenty, I'm sure. But should you focus on the field beyond, you'd see as well."

George looked and still didn't see anything. It wasn't until Imp put her hand on his shoulder that his vision seemed to snap into place. "You'll be able to see it with better eyes now. Do you see them?"

"Dragons. A lot of dragons."

There were too. With this new sight, he could see all of them. Camouflaged for the most part, but what got him the most was that they were flying above the ground with only a few inches between the earth and their feet. Uncle Cooper told him they did that so as not to alert anyone of their arrival.

"The humans, or even other creatures, would feel the earth moving beneath them. It would, most likely, bring many to see what the cause of it might be." They all watched as the first to arrive settled on his lawn. Great massive heads were lying there, large dragons that had only just arrived in a strange place. Ignis laughed. "They're trying very hard to figure out what to do, George. I would think you could easily give away eggs right now to make room for the many more that will have heard of what you're doing."

It wasn't as difficult to organize giving out the eggs as his mind made it. Helenia was a great deal of help. She told the dragons that were receiving eggs where the egg was found and what she could get from it with her touch. Everyone joined in the distribution of the eggs, and he thought it went very well.

"We should have kept track of the ones we gave out." Helenia said that Glacier had been doing it. George looked over the counts and was pleased with the results. "I wonder if this will be an occurrence all the time. With dragons showing up to get an egg."

"We'll take some with us on the morrow to take to those that are too far away to make the trip if you wish, my lord." No matter how many times he asked Helenia to just call him George, she still called him her lordship. "There will be aplenty left when we take them. I have noticed, as I'm sure you did, that the shelves where we took some out filled with more eggs."

"I was hoping I was seeing things." She didn't have much in the way of a sense of humor either. Not that she didn't laugh, she did, but she seemed to not get his sorry attempts at joking around with her. "I wasn't being truthful to you, Helenia. I'm just nervous that things won't go as planned. I'm so happy that we can get these young dragons to those that will help them."

"Aye, they will be well cared for. With the king here, they'll be doubly sure they care well for them." She looked at the last dragon to get an egg, tears flowing from his eyes as he took the large egg to his heart. "There will be aplenty of gems from them that will come back here for you to use. Once the hatchlings are born, there will be more. It is a good thing you'll be here for them when they need it most. The world, it will be a better place for all the magic that comes from this."

George knew that dragons were a reason for the magic of the world. What he'd not known, or perhaps not thought of, was how much magic a single dragon would have to use. It was enough to power the world, several times over, Imp had told him. And have plenty of it left over.

"She's right, you know. About the world being a better place. Those that believe will be able to see the dragons and those that would cause them harm will not. It's the magic I have given these that are in our care." George asked Imp what else she'd done for the eggs. "We'll be able to see them when they're hatched. A bit of magic will come to the dragon that cares for them. We'll need more land, of course, to raise the animals that will be needed to feed the little ones. Also, I did speak with the waterways, and where there will be a dragon staying, they'll make sure there are plenty of sea creatures to feed them. The water dragons too will be well cared for."

"When Helenia told me there were water dragons, I jokingly asked if it was that dragon like thing in Ireland. She just stared at me, like she does when she nods. I think she thinks I'm nuts." Imp told him he was. "Thank you ever so much for that. To think that I was going to take you up to our bedroom and ravage you for the rest of the night."

"As much as I would love that, I'm beyond exhausted." Now that he sat there with her, he could feel his own need for a peaceful night roll over him. "I just want to curl my body around yours and sleep until I wake. Even if it's a hundred years or so."

"I don't know about a hundred years, but I agree on getting some sleep." They walked hand in hand into their home. While they'd been working, the cook had fed them all when they could get into the house. But you'd never know it to look at the house. It was as spotless as he'd ever seen it. "I'm sort of hungry, but I don't have it in me to eat."

Bypassing the kitchen for bed, he was nearly up the stairs when he felt like he could easily sleep where he stood. It was Imp that got him going. As soon as his head hit the pillow, he was sure he blacked out. Exhaustion had never hit him this hard before.

~*~

Ignis watched the man at the hardware store. Yesterday he and George had come to the town and looked around. The opinion of the man had not improved on meeting him either. Jerry Benson was a first-class asshole. George had been right on the money when he suggested that the foundation buy up all the buildings he didn't own already and make some improvements there. Now the man was spouting off about how he'd been able to make a million and a half dollars from the sale of all the buildings he had supposedly owned.

George had made sure he met with all the business owners of the buildings he'd purchased yesterday, leaving not just his card but his personal cell number if they had any questions. He'd even let it be known that the bank had held the note on the buildings, not Benson. That had pissed off a great many people.

"He lorded it over us on how he was going to have to raise the rent on our place all the time. I swear to you, in the last six months or less, he'd

raised the 'rent' we were paying to near double."
George assured everyone that there would be no
more raises for the next five years. He also took
the amount they'd been paying five years ago as
payment enough. "That sure will help me out
in getting my son through college. Never seen
an expense so high in my life as getting a better
education."

"I agree with you on that one." George
gave those wanting them the email address of his
brother Hedley, who was helping college bound
people find a loan. And if that didn't work, a loan
from the foundation. "You call my brother there,
and he'll help you as much as he can. And what he
can't do for you — which I don't see as a problem
for him — he'll turn it over to my aunt and mom.
We'll help out as much as you need."

It had been like that all day, shaking hands
with the people around town. They'd even taken
their meals in a couple of homes of people they'd
met who needed more information, which Ignis
enjoyed too. The food was wonderful, and the
people were so nice to the two of them. But today
was a different story.

Benson had been run out of two storefronts
since ten that morning. Ignis would almost feel

sorry for the man, but he'd made his bed, and now he was going to have to lie in it. Or so the saying went. It wasn't as if he had stolen anything by saying he owned the buildings and collected the rent on them. But whatever he charged above the payment, he kept for himself. It was a tidy little profit too. Ignis moved closer to where the ice cream parlor was when he noticed that Imp was having herself a cone.

"He's not having a good day, I don't think. The man behind the counter in there told him that he wasn't going to save him a chicken sandwich anymore. I guess Benson made him do that in the event he wanted one later. They're very good. I've had four of them." He laughed when she offered him the last one on her plate. It was really good. "George wanted me to come here to make sure the town is doing all right. He thought you'd be here too and suggested that I bring Glacier. But she's helping with the eggs today and having so much fun. I needed a little break."

"George loves you." Imp said she loved him as well. "Yes, well, it's so wonderful to see someone besides Glacier and I love you. In a different way, of course, but he really is somewhat sappy around you."

"Yes, and I love him for that too. He calms me."

Ignis got up and ordered four more sandwiches for the two of them and some poppers. He hadn't any idea what they were but wanted to try some other things besides French fries. When he sat back down with his order, he handed one of the poppers to Imp while he shoved one in his own mouth.

To say that it was good would have been a total waste of words. It was fantastic. Like nothing he'd ever eaten before. The heat, a perfect mixture of the hot pepper and the hot cheese, made his head swim just a little. By the time he was on his third one, he'd concluded that his sister didn't care for them, and that would leave more for himself. Also, the man that had cooked them up for him had joined them at the table.

"You must really like it hot." Ignis told the man—Holly, his name was—that he loved the heat in all things. "You should go on down to my wife's shop. She has this pepper sauce that will melt your tongue. It's got them ghost peppers in it and some bits of tomato. Man, if I could eat that anymore, I'd be in heaven. My belly, it don't care for spicy since I had myself a heart attack some years back."

When he said that, Ignis noticed that Imp touched him. The shock to the man's system was evident, but he simply wrote it off as electrical waste, akin to something you'd get if you were to walk across a carpet and touch something, getting a little painless shock. As he sat there with them, it was him that got the man to try a little of the popper. In the end, the two of them shared three more servings of them.

"That man, Benson. He's a holy terror, he is. The reason I was laid up for so long with my heart troubles was on account of him." Imp asked Holly what had happened. "Come into my place one day telling me how I was going to be feeding his family from now on when they showed up. For free, he told me. Like I could afford to give him food when he came in for his daily offering. That's what he called it too. A daily offering, like he was some sort of king or something. Little bastard. But his family, four strapping boys, about done us in. Us thinking that if we didn't comply, he'd just raise the rent out of the price range we could afford and run us off. Thankfully he backed off when my missus called the police in. I don't know what we would have done hadn't she done that.

Then come to find out, he didn't own nothing. Not even his own car. Did you hear that he got that sucker repossessed today? The bank really jumped on him not being able to cash in on our woes."

They all three laughed about it as they enjoyed the afternoon sun. Ignis did love the outdoors and had forgotten what it was like to enjoy the company of a good man. Any person, he supposed. But he needed more information about a couple of things. He asked Holly what he knew about one of them.

"There was a school here about, oh, I'm thinking twenty years ago or so. About the time my oldest graduated from there." He looked pensive for a moment. "I don't know rightly what closed it down, but it was a big to-do. My wife, she'd know. I'll give her a call. She's got a woman that comes in and relieves her for a spell, so she'll be right down."

She did indeed show up. Ignis watched as merchant after merchant handed her things to put in her basket as she made her way to them. When she sat down, Belinda handed the basket to him and Imp. It was a gift from all the merchants.

"They're all so happy that Benson has been

handed his ass. Oh my, I was up to nearly midnight talking to Mrs. Joe about it. Said that it couldn't have happened to a meaner person." Imp asked her what else had happened. "Well, my dear, he's going to be voted off the town council for starters. Never did like him there telling us how things were going to go. Why, I have a good mind to go over to his home right now and tear up all the flowers in his yard that we had to plant for him. The Women's Committee, not the town. Not that he didn't make it difficult to get things done up for the town that way either. That's why we don't have a thing going on here anymore. Why, we used to have town picnics and the like. Ice cream socials. But he and that brood of his would come in and take gallons of ice cream home. Or pies and the like. After a while, none of us gave two nickels to just supply him with stuff, so it went by the wayside."

"What about the school? Holly said you'd remember what closed it down." She told him what she'd figured out and what she knew. "So he demanded a cut in the teachers' pay for supplying them with a place to work? How is that even legal?"

"I doubt that anyone looked too deeply into

it. Not that he had the police in his pocket, but he did bully them around enough that everyone was fearful of him. Or them boys of his." It was Imp that asked what he'd done to them. "One night, the sheriff and his family were run off the road. Nearly killed their youngest. One of them boys of his did it. The fires, too, that were started. The fire department, which is gone now too, couldn't be counted on to go help out since their tires were slashed up or the engine messed with. I don't know why he did such things. Don't know if we'll ever know, but Holly and me, I think like a lot of folks around here, were ready to throw in the towel with this town."

"You're not now?" Belinda said they were holding off. Just to see what come of George and his predictions of what he was going to do. "I know that as of this morning, he and his family have been looking into funding an elementary school building for this area. Also, the bus service will be up and going before too much longer. We didn't think about the fire department not being here, but I'll tell him when I talk to him next."

Ignis would bet anything that George had been told about the department and everything else that Belinda and Holly were telling them. He was almost certain the man would be working on it well past them coming back to the house.

Imp was writing things down that she was getting from the couple. A great many people came by to thank them for getting Benson taken care of. Really, all they'd done was take over the buildings, but it seemed that was enough for these people to start living again.

That was what it looked like to him as he looked around the town. There were children playing in the streets, moving out of the way when an occasional car came by. Women out on the park benches with their strollers with children and a dog or two. Ignis thought now that he knew he could pop in and see his sisters whenever he wanted, he'd like to make this place his home.

He owned a great deal of land that he could see himself building on around the world. Also, he'd like to raise some cattle, like the Duggar Ranch had. Not with deaths, however that had occurred when it was discovered that drugs were being sold and manufactured there. The scandal didn't seem to affect the people here at all. Thinking of it, he was ready to reach out to George again when he looked at his sister.

"You love it here, don't you?" He looked at

his sister and realized that at some point, they'd been left alone. "You're going to leave us and move here, aren't you?"

"I think I am." She didn't beg him to stay, which meant she thought it was a good idea as well. "Knowing I can see you and Glacier anytime I want makes it easier on me to make the decision. How on earth did you find the ranch so far from your home?"

"Looking for a lost wolf. Flying overhead, it's not really that far. It's the driving here that would take forever, I think. Hours and hours by the way the roads flow." He asked her if she thought he could make it. "Make it? I'm not sure if you realize this or not, Ignis, but you've been making it all your life."

He laughed. She did as well, but he could feel the sadness that she was having. It wasn't going to be like that, he assured her. They'd be closer than ever since they could use their magic to visit.

"Glacier would come here to live with you. Maybe cramp your style a little, but she would do it. This place needs her around. You, too, to bring it from the brink of disaster. It was nearly there, you know." He nodded and looked around again. "The school is being taken care of. It's far enough on the outskirts of town that George had the faeries go and get it ready for the next school year. There will be people here in a few days to look over the fire department and see what it will need to get up and running. Even the bank, which we don't really need, is helping out as much as it can with lower interest rates for the money being used."

"I'm going to talk to George and you tonight about the Duggar Ranch. As you said, it's not nearly as far away as it looks on a map. Not for us. I'd like to run the ranch raise some cows and sheep for the dragons to eat. Also, I've got an idea that I can blend my properties with it, as I think they're all close enough that a few dragons could come to stay there as well." She slid an envelope across the table at him. Opening it, he laid it back on the table and smiled at her. "This is the deed to the place. How did you know?"

"I didn't. George told me you kept talking about the place yesterday with him. And that you were talking about the amount of food that could be raised there to help out. He talked to his uncle and the rest of the family last night, and they agreed with him on it being the perfect place for you to help us out. I'm not sure anyone thought of you having dragons here. But I can see it as a good place for them to be." He asked if she'd miss him. "Yes. I miss you right now. But as we said earlier, it's only a matter of popping in to see you. And you'd better make sure I have about a dozen of these chicken sandwiches when I come by too."

"I'll do that for you and George." He looked at the couple that was sharing their ice cream with a small child. "Do you suppose you'll have children with George? He's a good man. I love him like a brother."

"And he loves you too, Ignis." She laughed, and he asked her what was so funny. "Us. Not two weeks ago, we were sad and depressed that we didn't get to see each other anymore. Now here we are, you're going to be moving here, and I'll be raising dragons with George. I also know that Glacier will come here. Perhaps not with you on the ranch, but I suspect if you ask her, she would just to live near you. The two of you were so close when we were together. I was jealous for a time. Then I realized that you were my family, and to be jealous of you and Glacier together was silly. I loved what we were up to all the more for that realization."

"When you were being particularly cranky, as you so wrongfully called it, I'd go find Glacier to unburden on her how much you irritated me. She'd tell me that you were getting the job done, and I'd feel better. Right up until you were cranky again with her." He cocked his head and looked at Imp, seemingly for the first time. "You're calmer. No, that's not it. You're mellow. No, that's not it either. You're something. Different is all I can think of."

"I'm in love." They both stood up, and she told him that his house was finished. "The faeries were only waiting on my signal to go there and clean the place up. The police, or whatever agency Carson deals with, has finished with it, and there will not be any traces of the activities that had been going on. Glacier is waiting there for you as well. For you to tell her which rooms she can have so, she can take the ones she wants."

Hugging her now was so natural that he hung onto her for a little longer. When she pulled back, he looked at her. Christ, how did he miss how beautiful she was? And Imp was. When her face brightened, she pulled the rest of the way out of his arms and smiled at him.

"Carson said to tell you that you have a mate

coming and that you'd better not fuck it up with her. Glacier has a mate coming to her soon, but later." Ignis told her he didn't want a mate. "Well, isn't that just too fucking bad? You have one, and she's coming. If you do fuck this up, Ignis, I will hurt you."

"I have no intentions of messing anything up. I might, however, go back to my caves to get away from an impending mate. What the hell would I do with a mate anyway?" Imp was still laughing when she walked away. "Imp? Did she tell you when this was going to happen? Imp, I'm speaking to you."

The dog knocked him to his ass as soon as his sister disappeared. It was a mangy looking mutt, and he was ready to help it become a better looking pup when a little boy tackled him to his back. They stared at one another as if they were new to using their eyeballs. Setting the boy aside, the puppy started bathing his face like he had a tasty treat on it.

"Stop." The dog sat down and didn't move. The little boy looked like he had taken the command too. He wasn't moving either. "I meant the dog. Where did you get that thing?"

"Mr. Benson was going to cut his head off

and serve it to me." Ignis had to have heard that wrong, but the little boy nodded. "I took him outta there in a minute. Then I fell back there and skinned up my knee. I know we can't afford a dog right now, but I'll give him scraps until we can."

He opened his mouth to tell the little boy that he'd help him so the dog could eat better, and him if necessary when he was suddenly being yelled at by a woman standing over them both. Ignis had no doubt that this was the boy's mother, and she was scared for him.

"He's all right." Ignis asked the boy his name. "Dwayne is all right. So is the mutt. Mr. Benson is not going to get his hands on either of them."

"He will too. He doesn't like us anyway." Ignis stood up with her help, knowing after her hand left his what she was to him. "Benson seems to think because I'm a widow that I should... well, I don't. And he isn't going to make me do a damned thing."

His mate, Danielle Skinner, was just like his sisters. Mouthy, protective, and beautiful. Talking her into coming out to the ranch with him, he was surprised at the ease he was having talking to her. Glacier was there to take the pup and the boy into the house.

    As they sat out on the porch together, talking about everything and anything, Ignis thanked his sister. Her laughter was all he needed to know that he was going to be as happy as she was. Forever.

Chapter 7

Running her hand along the stone, she knew that whatever she was feeling wasn't right. Well, that was an understatement, Imp thought. She'd been able to read stones before. But it was more that she could feel its pain or whatever she wanted from it. Nothing like Finn did or his wife. Turning to look at George, she wasn't sure if he was being sappy again or making fun of her. Either way, she dearly loved him.

"It's not talking to me. It's being stupid and mean. What the fuck am I supposed to do when it's being like—it's a man rock, isn't it? The entire male population is stubborn." That, of course, set George and his brother Hedley off in fits of laughter. "What am I supposed to do?"

"You don't need to caress it, Imp. If it is a male stone, then he's probably waiting to come all over your hand." George was too blunt. Hedley fell to the ground, his mirth getting the better of him. Kicking him in the booted foot, she demanded that he get up while George continued. "According to Finn, they're neither gender or both. I doubt very much that it's going to start having fantasy sex now."

"Oh, do be quiet." She turned to look at the stone, fighting hard not to laugh herself. Touching just her fingers to the stone, all sorts of things racing around in her head, she felt the stone speak. Or something like a language, she supposed. "I can hear it rumbling or something. But I don't know what it's saying. Now I have to learn a new language too?"

I will speak to you. She put her hand on the stone when it spoke to her. *You are the creator of dragons. I was shocked that one so wonderful as you would speak to a lowly rock such as myself.*

"You're not lowly anything. I should like it if you were to not think that again. Without you and the other stones, how would the mountains be sturdy enough to hold such magnificent beasts as my dragons? Where would we go when we wished to take in the splendor of the view of trees turning in the fall? Or the spring flowers that grow plentiful around here? Nay, my stone friend, without you, the world would be nothing but flat surfaces that would be boring even to the most unhappy of a person. You're not lowly, but one of the greatest additions to the world as a whole." He thanked her. "I wish I didn't have to disturb you, but I do have a question I think only you can answer for me. We're looking for the bones of a great dragon. The ones we're searching for, they are said to be that of Ava, the Jade dragon. Faeries long ago hid her inside the mountains so her body wouldn't be ravaged by humans set to take her apart."

I know I do hold some bones behind my back, my lady, but I haven't any idea who they belong to. Ava the Jade was a good person. Her mate, Coop the Red, was a great leader and a good dragon to those he ruled. She told him she was mated to one of his grandsons. That his father was Xavier, the youngest. *Oh, what a rare and wonderful treat for myself. I shall be the envy of all that hear this story. Yes, and when I tell the story, I will inquire about bones that might be hidden in other mountains. To have them put to rest, it will be a good thing for so many others.*

"I agree. How can I figure out how to get to the resting place without causing complaint to you or those around you? These trees, they look as if they've been sheltering you for a long time. I don't want anyone to be hurt by this move." He told her that he could move enough for her to see that she could get inside. "You mean magically. Yes, that would be perfect. I don't want to pop into a stone or anything else that might hurt myself."

The stone moved, and she turned to tell George and Hedley what was going on. The two of them were staring at her as if she had...well, just spoken to a stone. Asking them what was wrong, Hedley just shook his head, and George stood up to hold her.

"Finn only gets images from stone. He has gotten really good at figuring out what the stones are telling him that way. But you, you just had an entire conversation with one, and he not only understood what you were saying, but you him. I'm impressed with you more and more daily. And I don't think I could love you any more than I do right now." She thanked him and asked him why with this. "Because, love, you were first concerned about the stone and what would happen should it be moved. Then you were concerned for yourself.

That is the way a true lover of the earth would think."

"Thank you. So much." They used flashlights to see inside of the darkness. "I will go in. Not that you couldn't as well, but I've been doing this longer than you, and I can be more precise as to where I need to be. I don't think it's going to be dangerous in there. I think the stone would have said so."

"I agree with you. However, I'd like to go in with you at some point. There is nothing I'd like better than to see my grandmother's resting place should this be her. The faeries seemed quite sure this was the mountain, correct?" She smacked her hand to her forehead. "What? You've thought of something?"

"The faeries can go in this opening and see into the darkness better than anyone. I didn't even think of that. I can send them in to have a look around and then tell us if this is her. We'll still bring the bones out, but the little people will be safer inside than any one of us will be." George thought that was a good idea. "I have them on occasion. All right. We'll call to them and see which one is brave enough to go inside the darkness."

There were no numbers that she could

count to for the number of faeries that wanted to go and do this for them. She finally had to have a group of them going inside for one minute each so they could say they were a part of it. Even that took about three hours. The stone thought it the funniest thing that had ever happened to him. Imp thought he was enjoying the to-do more than anyone would have thought a stone could.

There was enough light now inside with the magic, so she took a look inside the deep darkness beyond. Nothing. She could feel or see nothing beyond the entrance. It wasn't until the last group, the most senior faeries, went in that the resting place of Ava the Jade was found.

All manner of creatures came to help with her being taken to the property of Cooper and Carson Manning. To say it was a somber affair would have been grossly understated. No one, not even those born or hatched after her death, wasn't affected by the removal.

Tears were shed for her being no more. Flower petals were tossed upon the bones that had been separated to be moved. The little ones that carried their responsibility were solemn as well. Their burden, one that had been long in finding, was something that legend had told about. Ava the Jade had given her life for her six hatchlings the day she was taken from this world. A sacrifice by the greatness of love.

Imp spread magic over the bones as they were being brought out. The magic would preserve the bones more, taking away some of the decay that had been set upon them. When George took her hand into his, she felt his sadness all the way to her heart. She had known Ava the Jade— he had only heard long ago stories about her.

"The day she was taken, I saw her fall. There was little to nothing I could do for her. Her wounds were too great. Almost the moment she landed in the valley, several miles from where she had been felled, the humans were upon her." George asked the warrior fae what her name was. "Milly, my lord. I am Milly, the rider for her. She'd been a good dragon to me and my family. Even before she was taken. I shall never forget her or the ride I had for such a short time. I wished to also give you this."

It was a scale from her body. As big as she was. Imp turned it when she saw what had been carved into it and showed it to George. It was an image of the great dragon with eggs spread out around her. Along with her face, smiling at her brood, there were gems of every color around her and her babies.

"This is beautiful. I cannot accept such a gift. You should keep it." Milly backed away from the scale, saying she had others of her likeness that she loved almost as much. "This is the first time I've seen such workmanship, Milly. You must have loved my grandmother a great deal."

"I did, my lord. We all did."

When Milly walked away, George looked at Imp. He was crying again, his face wet with the tears that were turning into jade. He asked her to send it to Cooper's home.

"I can do that. I don't think he should take it, but I'll send it on." He said he was the king of dragons. "Yes, he is. And you're the grandson, no matter your birth, of my first dragons. You and your brothers need things like this as much as he does. Because no matter how you look at it, George, without her, without Coop, you would never have been. Never have been there when I needed you. Any of us needed you. You tell him if he has a problem with you keeping this, he should come to talk to me. I'll set his ass right."

Going to their home first, they gathered up the things they'd need to set things right for

Ava. Coop's body had been removed several days beforehand, and there was going to be a great ceremony once they were both put to rest. Dawn was there to make sure things went well, and she was going to give her blessing on the place that the couple would be placed.

It would forever bloom with flowers and other living things. Snow would never cover the blooms. Nothing would be able to enter the circle made for them. No one would be able to disturb the peace surrounding the faerie garden either.

"When they're set to rest, Ignis is going to bring a stone he's carved for them. It will only say that Coop and Ava Manning are residing there." Cooper nodded at Imp as they were all standing around the still area near the garden. "I have added my own magic to this place as well. The images that I have of the two of them will be here should anyone wish to see them. All they will need to do is say is their names."

"Thank you for that. Our children will know the likeness of the two of them forevermore. You've...well, I cannot think of any words that convey my thankfulness for you looking for and finding her for us. I know that my dad had been taken away the day of the magic, but I didn't know until recently that our mother's body hadn't been. To know that they're together again, it's too... thank you, Imperium Manning." Imp walked back to where George stood and hugged him.

As soon as the bodies were laid beneath the rich soil, flowers began to come up and bloom. In a matter of seconds, it looked as if the area had been there for decades rather than only a few seconds. When Imp told her brother that it was finished, he and Danielle, his mate, stepped forward. The stone that was to lay over their hearts was as beautiful as anything she'd ever seen.

"Glacier put the ice vases on the side. They shan't melt, but if there are flowers within them, they will be watered until they are taken away or replaced." They all thanked them both. "My sister Imp has added the magic that will forever bring them to life for those that wish it. A bench, made by all the woodland creatures, will be placed once we have all moved away. This place will forever be called Manning. Nothing more needs to be said, as it will be a place of great reverence and love."

When the ceremony was over, the Mannings shook hands and hugged as many people as they could. Danielle came to stand next to her and took her hand into hers too. She was happy. Imp could tell. And her little boy was getting better by the day.

"I didn't know he'd been sick." Imp told her sister-in-law that she'd not touched him, so she didn't either. "Ignis healed him. Told me that if it had waited much longer, like only a few weeks, he would have been gone. I don't know how you knew that Ignis and I were mates, but I will be forever grateful for you. And I have to tell you, Glacier is the best aunt to him. Even Mr. Trouble, the stupid dog that took Ignis down, loves to be around her."

She told her that Carson, who could see a little of the future, had told her.

"And you? Do you like living on the ranch with Ignis and the other creatures?" Her face told her that she did indeed love living there. "I'm glad you're both so happy, Danielle. You and Ignis are going to be so helpful in the hatching of dragons. Thank you for understanding."

"Understanding? Oh, honey, I don't understand any of this, but I'm getting there. However, while I'm riding this rainbow of information, I get to hang out with dragons and faeries. Brownies help around the house. We have money to burn, which I will not do, but it's nice to know that we, Dwayne and I, will never be hungry again. And that we'll both be loved beyond anything we've ever imagined. I have two sisters that I didn't before, a roof over my head, and my heart so full it's almost like a dream." Danielle looked at Ignis. "I know the fates will match two people that deserve each other. But I have to admit I think I got the better end of the deal with Ignis and the rest of you. Being loved like this, it's something that so few gets to experience."

"Yes, I agree with you there." They were walking back to the house when Danielle left her to get her son from Carson. She'd adopted him as her great-grandson, it seemed. She went to talk to Cindi, her mother-in-law. "I have a job for you, Cindi. One that I think only you can do for me."

"Whatever it is, consider it done." She told her not to be so hasty. "I don't think you'd have me do anything that would harm me. No, you'd not do that. Nor would you ask me to do something that would upset the family. So again, whatever you wish, it's yours."

She told her about the scale and what it looked like, telling her that it had been given to George as a gift for finding Ava. Cindi asked what she thought she could do about that. Nodding, she touched her forehead so she could see an image of the artwork.

"Oh my, that's beautiful, and you say she has more?" Imp told Cindi she didn't think she wanted to part with those. "No, of course not. I can understand that. What is it you need for me to do for you? If it has to do with Cooper trying to lay claim to it, you can bet your sweet ass I'm going to stand up for my son. Not only that, but I'll hurt him badly if Cooper tries it."

"I don't know that he will want it. I mean, he is the first born. But I think I might have something to appease him if he should want it." She handed her an emerald as big as her head. "It's theirs. Ava and Coop's. I didn't know what it was until later. Ignis and Glacier had added to the magic that created the dragons, and that was their part. Love producing an emerald."

"I don't think I've ever seen an emerald this big before." She told her why it was so large. "Oh, Imp. That is the most romantic story I think ever told. Their love for each other and their children are all in this one gem. Yes, I can see the marks now where they were blended together."

"If you look at it closely, you can also see

the bits of eggs from each of their six boys when they were hatched." Turning the stone over, she pointed out each of the pieces for the other woman. "I'm not sure how they were able to do that, I have a feeling my brother and sister helped, but it's something he can have in replacement for the scale."

"If he puts up a fuss, I'm going to shove this up his ass. Then make him shit it out. I'm sure that both times will be painful enough that he'll reconsider your plan." Imp loved this woman and told her so. "And I love you, my dear Imp. I couldn't have asked for better daughters for my sons. But you, you and your family have brought us so much that I think no matter what happens from now on, I know that you've given your all to us, and then some."

~*~

George could see that his uncle was torn. He wanted them both, the gem and the scale. However, his mom had made it perfectly and painfully clear that he was only going to get one. And that he'd better pick the gem, or he was going to be in a great deal more pain in the very near future. When he handed him the scale — the sucker was as large as Uncle Cooper — Mom handed him the gem. Then she told him what was inside the gem.

"You could have told me that in the beginning, you know." Mom asked him why he thought that would have been fun for her. "Are you ever going to give me the respect I so rightly deserve as your king?"

"Nope. And if you think that is going to happen after all this time, you're dumber than the post holding up your front porch." Mom kissed his uncle and smiled up at him. "I have to be honest with you, Cooper. I was hoping you'd choose the wrong one. Or take them both. I know you could have, and we would have let you. However, I would have made your life a living hell. All of us would."

"Again, telling me that a part of each of us was in the gem would have solved this easily. You're forever making things difficult for me." She said it was a perk she loved of being a Manning. "You're not right in the head. I hope you know that."

"I have to put up with you, so that's a given. Enjoy the gem, Cooper, and thank your nephew — once again — for giving you a piece of your mother and father. I would think you'd have something better than a simple thank you — again — since you have them both here and he did the most work with his mate. You're slacking if you ask me."

Mom walked away, and Uncle Cooper turned to look at him.

"I didn't put her up to that." He said he knew that. Then he laughed. "You think it's funny that my mom is giving you a hard time? I was afraid for you. I know how she can get."

"I love your mom because she doesn't bow before me. Even if she did, I'd be looking for some kind of trickery from her." Uncle Cooper put his hand on his shoulder before speaking again. "I do have something for you. I've had it since you gave me the teapot. Here you go."

The sword he handed him was long and beautifully crafted. The pommel was decorated with all the gems he could name and some he couldn't. When he asked him where it had come from, Uncle Cooper took him into the living room where he could show him. He asked for the images of his parents to be brought up.

The images of his parents came up as they did when Imp had done it. George was getting better at his magic and was surprised at the ease in which he was able to do it. Shaking his head,

Uncle Cooper asked him if he could go back to another time when Xavier, his brother, was fighting in a war.

"Stop." George wasn't sure what he was looking at until his uncle stood up. "There. Do you see it, George? It's the sword I have given you in your father's hand. It was given to him by a great woman the day before, you see. Xavier had been out and about when he heard a woman screaming. He managed to save her with his bare hands from the men who had decided to hold her hostage so the king of the castle would leave without incident. Of course, it didn't happen that way, but the sword was given to Xavier, and he was knighted with it as well. It has long since been in the cave we own, and I had one of the faeries look for it."

"This should go to one of my brothers, Uncle Cooper." He asked him why he'd think that. "Well, for one thing, they're older than me. Secondly, I'm not a dragon, nor was I born a—"

"Don't you dare say that. Don't you sit there and tell me you're not a Manning. Since the day you were brought to this family, you've been a Manning and nothing more. You might not have been born a dragon, George, but you're as much dragon as I am as far as I'm concerned. You've gone well beyond anything that anyone ever expected of you. And this, what you've done for me, is something no one has ever thought to do before. I don't want you to think that simply because you were adopted, you're any less than Xavier's hatchlings are. You have never been, nor will you ever be. You're a Manning. And you're my family. Take the damn sword before I knock you on your ass with it."

When he smiled, George let out a long breath before Uncle Cooper told him to wait a moment. The others gathered in the room. While he didn't know what was going on, he was thinking Uncle Cooper wouldn't hurt him with so many witnesses. Asking for the sword again, he asked him to get down on one knee. It was then that Imp took the sword from Uncle Cooper and smiled at him.

"This is epic." Imp cleared her throat when Ignis and Glacier appeared beside her, each of them putting their hand on the sword. "As creator of dragons and mate to George Manning, we hereby give you the title that you so richly deserve. You are now and forever will be known as George Manning, Lord of Manning Castle.

Protector of artifacts. George the Emerald. Father of all hatchlings."

The moment the sword touched his shoulder, he knew that something was going to happen. It might not be the epic that Imp said, but it was something huge. Falling back on the floor, he felt something run from his nose and knew he was bleeding. Why? He didn't have a clue. There wasn't any pain, not really, just a great deal of stretching and movement of his internal body.

When he sat up, he was in the bed he shared with Imp, and she was lying next to him. When he moved to touch her, she opened her eyes and smiled at him. He asked her how long he'd been out. And why?"

"Four days. Which I have to tell you is a great deal less than your dumbass uncle said it would be. Why is he even king? He can't get shit right. Anyway. After I knighted you and gave you the gift, I did the same for Milo." He asked her what she'd done. "Oh, you're both dragons."

She got out of bed like that wasn't anything important. "What do you mean, we're both dragons? I was born a human." Imp told him he'd not been a human for a very long time. "I know that. But how am I a dragon? And I'm assuming since you called me Emerald that my dragon is an emerald. What is going on? Did Uncle Cooper put you up to this?"

"Yes, he asked me if I could do it for you and your brother, and I did. I did create dragons, you know. It wasn't hard, not with the help of my —" He growled at her. "See there. That was magnificent. But back to you being a dragon. If you were to get your lazy ass out of bed, we can go out into the yard, and you can shift into him. By the way, as far as I know, you're the only living emerald dragon. Milo is sapphire. He's still resting."

He was alone in the room when she yelled at him to get out of bed. Staggering just a little, he was dressed and down the stairs in record time, he thought. However, Imp was in the yard waiting for him, and she didn't look like she was pleased that he was taking so long.

"I've never done this before." Imp told him it was a simple thing. He only needed to think of his dragon, then he'd be there. "That's all?"

Before he could even imagine what it was going to be like to be a dragon, he was standing over Imp. Far, far over her. Lying down on the grass near her, he remembered all the things he'd heard his family say when they were a dragon.

"I need to keep telling myself that you're my George." He told her, through their link, that he wasn't sure what he was at the moment. "I have an image of you in my mind should you like to see yourself. Also, this might not be a big deal to you, but as a dragon, your eyes are like the darkest of emeralds."

This is surreal for me. All my life, I've been envious of my brothers for being able to shift into a dragon. I think I'm going to miss all the other perks you gave me. She asked him what he meant. *You know, popping in and out of places. Being able to use the elements that you can. Little stuff that seems silly to think about now that I've said them out loud.*

"You can still do all that. More, I would imagine. I don't know that I'd try popping in someplace right now as a dragon, but I'm betting you can do that as well. It would be a good thing to wait a couple of weeks on that. We'd have to find a place large enough to hold you." He laughed. George hadn't ever felt this good. "Don't move just yet."

When she came to him, sitting on one of his outstretched arms, he was as content as he'd ever been. As she began to relax, he did as well. George knew now why it was so freeing to be a dragon.

"I love you so much, George." He told her he loved her as well. "I don't know that we'll have children. I don't know anything about my body to give you that information. But I'd like to adopt too. To give kids like you were a chance at life. I don't know a great deal about kids, only in that you have to keep them safe and shit like that, but we'll figure it out. Your mom, I think she'd be a great help for me too."

Mom will be in heaven if you tell her what you just told me. She nodded—he could feel the movement as she did it. *I will do whatever I can to make you happier every day. I love you so very much.*

They stayed in the yard for another hour. He had shifted back to himself at some point, and they still sat outside in the waning light. When they finally made their way into the house, Imp took the shell and put it over the mantel. That was when he asked her about the Castle Manning.

Chapter 8

"You said castle." Imp turned and looked at him. "You mentioned that I was the lord of Manning Castle. Is that something that was in my family as well? I don't think I've ever heard anyone mention it before."

"It's ours. Well, I had it before I met you, obviously. I did live in it for a time. I sometimes go there when I need a dose of just being around magic. It's very magical." George asked her where it was. "Want to go there? We can make a day or two of it. There is Internet, as well as anything else you'd likely need if you wanted to work. I know you have some things you're working on for the family."

"I do. Not a great deal. I— Yes, I'd love to

go. Whatever is here, it can wait for a couple of days. And if we stay longer, that's something we can work on when that time comes. What do we need to bring with us?" She told him she'd have to let Aster know, and things would be taken care of. "Great. The sooner, the better so no one thinks of something we can be doing."

He'd noticed a couple of days ago that Imp's faerie had been replaced with Aster. While he wasn't worried about the changes, as he'd seen the little faerie around, he did wonder where this new one came from. He needed to get himself another faerie as well. One that could help a dragon.

Every time he thought about being a dragon, he had to pinch himself. He'd not mention that part around Imp again. She pinched him hard enough that his dragon would shy away from her when she had that look in her eye. The "Why do I have to prove shit to you all the time?" look.

"All right. It's set up. It'll be ready when we arrive. Do you have to tell anyone that we'll be gone? I mean, they can still bother you if they need something." He laughed when she pouted. "Well, you have to admit, Cooper has been coming by a good deal more than necessary. And if he thanks me one more time, I'm going to take his dragon away from him for an hour. That should cap his ass. By the way, did you know your brother is having a good time with his dragon as well? Jamie said she has to beg him to come into the house as a person now. But I bet it wears off soon."

"I don't think I'd count on it being anytime too soon. I know just how he feels. If I didn't have work, I might be tempted to do the same. It's the strangest feeling being something so very much larger than you are as a human. It's like being reborn into magic, I think." She said she'd not thought of it like that. "Heady, I guess you'd call it too. But also, I find it unnerving a little. I have to be so careful about moving, stepping. I'm sure as I get used to it, I'll relax a little, but the thought of crushing something or hurting anyone or anything scares me too."

"You're very tense as a dragon until you're lying down. I know you've not flown yet, but I think your tension will lessen when you do that. *That* is a heady feeling. Seeing things from a perspective that very few people can accomplish." She moved into the kitchen, and he followed her. "We're set to stay the night. However, it won't be an issue if we decide to stay longer. Forever, I mean."

"I don't know that we'll be able to do that. Since I guess we could go there and come back as necessary, we could do that." He'd do anything to make Imp as happy as she seemed to be of late. "I'm also not going to tell anyone that we're going away. That way, they can't think of things to hit us with when we return. If we return."

Not returning was sounding better the more George thought of it. Not that he wouldn't, but for now, all he wanted to do was spend a few hours just not having to do a damned thing. The computer stuff he was doing for the family wasn't piling up right now. He wasn't on a deadline, not yet, at any rate. And if anyone really needed him, he'd be able to talk to them, from wherever they were going. George was also hoping it was far enough away so no one would be able to just drop by.

As they were getting ready to leave, George did decide to tell his parents. They were known for just dropping by for something or even nothing at all at times. They didn't stay long, but he didn't want them to worry, especially his mom.

You guys have fun then. I'll keep everyone from contacting the two of you too. Make sure you take pictures, George. I'd love to see what the castle looks like. He promised his mom he'd do that for her. *Good. Then I'll tell you now how much I missed you both. Because you know I will.*

I love you, Mom. So much. Yes, I'll make sure I find you the moment we're back. But don't be worried if it's not for a couple of days. I think we need this more than anything. And Helenia has been running the eggs out with her team. It's not nearly as crowded as it was at the beginning. There were still a great many eggs to have to distribute, but it wasn't as overwhelming as it had been. He thought it could have been because they were getting a method of doing it down better. *Once the two of us return, I'll be buckling down and getting to work.*

George, you're forever working. Just have some fun with that pretty mate of yours. She's a pistol, I have to tell you that. I never understood the meaning until she came along. I think Imp outdoes Carson at times, and you know she's a handful. They both laughed, telling his mom he thought so as well. *All right then. You relax, and we'll get together for dinner when you return. And you'd better return happy and relaxed. Sated too, if I know that girl of yours.*

Embarrassed, he told Imp what his mother had said. She was still laughing when they walked to the tree line of their yard. Confused a little, he was surprised when she walked into the deep woods. Right behind her all the way, he could almost feel the tension in his shoulders and neck disappearing with each step they took.

When Imp stopped in front of a large tree, he wanted to just sit under it, let the leaves that were beginning to turn fall over him and enjoy the animals that would be coming out soon. He'd never been one that just enjoyed the moment. Stopping to smell the roses, so to speak. But right now, with Imp by his side, he thought he could do just that.

"We're here." He looked around. Nothing was around them that even remotely looked like a castle. "I have it hidden from prying eyes. It's easier to escape when no one knows where to look for you. Don't you agree?"

"I do. So, do we just pop there or something?" She walked to the tree he'd been admiring for holding him up. When she touched her fingers to the bark, just above the knothole, the tree lit up. Each space between the long lines of bark seemed to come alive with blue and green lights. As soon as the door opened, Imp stood back. "You're not going to shove me in here, leaving me to be all alone for the rest of my life, are you, love?"

"I'd never leave you anywhere. At any time. Life would be nothing without you in it." Turning to the door that led to her realm, he was sure of that, Imp entered, and he followed. Whatever he expected, and he really didn't have any expectations at all, what he was seeing was about as indescribable as anything he'd ever seen. "It's beautiful, isn't it?"

"Beautiful? Christ, Imp, it's magnificent. And huge. I didn't know what to expect, but this... this is surreal. It's like it's in another dimension. Are we?" She told him where they were. "So this tree, it's not real, but a portal to this place. I love it. I'm assuming it's something like Dawn has with her castle."

"Yes, exactly. I told her how to do it so she'd not be out where people could accost her. At the beginning, that's what was going on with her. It's much easier for her now to be able to get out of sight. We'll have to visit Ignis's home underground. He has a beautiful antebellum home that is behind a large stone. Some of the furniture in it is true to the period too. Oh, and Glacier's place. From the outside, it looks like it's a lean-to that will fall over in a soft wind. But inside, it's as large as Cooper's home." He asked her if they were going to do that to their home. "If you'd like. But having this home here, we can get away and not have the same things around us. I love it here."

They talked about all the features the castle had that she had put in. Indoor plumbing, for one thing. When she'd started out, there wasn't anything like that. There was also electricity, cable, and Internet. No humans were working or living in the castle, as it was pure magic. Imp explained to him what that meant.

"Once you enter, you'll see what I mean more. It feeds off your magic, and then when you need more, it will give it back to you. You being a dragon will help all the household here. The people that work here, they're all creatures of the earth." As he entered the castle, the large drawbridge down for their arrival, a raccoon greeted them at the door. "This is, of course, Bandit. He picked his own name, and that was it."

"Good day, my lady. The household is awaiting you in the kitchen to meet the new lord." They followed the raccoon while he held onto a small computer and gave them the information he had for them. "Dinner will be salmon on the grill. We're to have fresh green beans as well as a heavy bread. For dessert, I've had the cook put together a nice sherbet with fresh berries. I hope that is all right?"

"Yes, of course." They entered the kitchen. George nearly backed out, thinking he was most assuredly in the wrong part of the house. "I'd like for everyone to meet my mate and best friend, George Manning of the Manning dragons. I hope everyone got the information on the name change here."

There were goats that stood on their hind legs while leaning against the table. A large cockatoo was standing on the back of one of the chairs that were currently holding what he could only assume was a troll. Everywhere he looked, there were animals he knew about as well as ones he had only heard about. A unicorn—Gerald, it turned out—was the butler for the castle.

After being shown around to the seemingly endless number of rooms, he was ready to go out on the deck and enjoy the afternoon with Imp. There was a hot tub on the deck, as well as a pool that was the same warm temperature all the time. Even the weather, which she had decided was a nice summery day, was kept that way through climate control.

"It rains at night, so the flowers and such

can be watered. The trees do go through the fall-like changes, but they're only bare for a couple of weeks before they start over again. When I was very depressed, a great deal of the time toward the end before meeting you, I'd avoid this place. It's painful to see the nakedness of them when you're already down." He said one of his aunts had suffered from depression as well. "When I was contacted during the bank robbery when I found out about your uncle, I was ready to go to him and get him to remove my head. He could have done it. However, now that I've met him, I'm betting he wouldn't have done it. I'm so happy I didn't go there that day with the thoughts of having him end my life."

"You have no idea how happy I am that you didn't have him do it." They sat on loungers, side by side, so that they could touch each other. Drinks and fruit appeared on the little tables on either side of them. George was happy to see that he had some tuna sushi as well. As a dragon now, he needed more protein.

He napped off and on. Twice he woke to find Imp in the yard with someone. Once, it was a larger version of the troll in the house. The second time it was a group of winged creatures. When she returned that time, he asked her if everything was all right.

"It is. They have a gift for you." George sat up on the chair and stared at the group, telling her he didn't need anything. "Perhaps, but you must take it. They've been waiting for me to return for some time now and are thrilled that there is a lord of the household. They're fae too. Fae have a thing for males being head of household. The gift is a bit of magic."

"Do I need more magic?" She laughed and waved the people over. After being introduced to the family, as it turned out, he was handed a medium sized basket of fruit. "What sort of fruit is this?"

He had meant to ask Imp, but the male of the group, Honduras, was the one that answered. "'Tis a cross between an apple and a peach, my lord. The magic within them is from the fae nation. A place where the purest magic comes from."

Taking a bite of the fruit, he was surprised by the wonderful flavor. Imp told him, through their link, that all the people here thought they were the purest form of magic. When he finished the fruit, handing the seed back to Honduras, they were happy, he supposed and left them.

"Don't eat too many of them. One every other day is more than enough for you to get magic from them. If you eat too many, like even just two, you're going to have diarrhea for a week." He nearly snorted his tea, glass and all, up his nose when she said that. "And don't let that pretty light color fool you into thinking you won't be shitting out green either. Christ, I thought I'd died when that happened the first time."

George was still laughing when they made their way into the living room later. They were sitting on the couch watching a football game when he realized how good he felt. Not just being relaxed, he realized, but he was energized and ready to take on whatever came his way. It wasn't until someone woke him for dinner that he realized how false that feeling had been. He wasn't as rested as he had thought he was when at their other home. This place was going to be good for him. For the two of them.

~*~

Toby hung up the phone when she didn't find a phone number for George Manning. She didn't know why she thought the man could help her, but since her uncle had finally been arrested, she was going to go out on a limb and find out if he knew what he'd gotten in the way of the pretty teapots. Also, she was told he'd gotten the handless cups that had gone with it.

Being the one that had covered the teapot in the clay, she wanted to make sure he knew what a treasure it was that he'd purchased. The fact that he got it for such an ungodly low amount thrilled her to no end. People like her uncle, Donald Deaver, were better off not being born.

Just as she was getting ready to call it a day, she saw a couple walking down the street across from her. Toby wasn't sure how she thought it was a Manning or even why she did, but she crossed the street at the light. As soon as she stepped in front of the two of them, she felt the hairs on the back of her neck dance.

"You're not human." Neither of them said anything, but they did stiffen a little. "I know you have no idea who I am or that you should care, but I'm the niece of Donald Deaver. My name is Toby Deaver. I want to say up front that I'm glad he was finally arrested. However, I do have some information on one of the teapots you purchased."

"Why is it you think that we purchased anything from your uncle, Toby?" The woman wasn't nasty, but Toby would bet in a second that she could be if crossed. "My name is Imp Manning. This is my mate, George. He's a dragon since you know we're not human, so I'd watch my next words if I were you."

Nodding, she said that she would. "How did I know? Well, you're not going to believe me, or perhaps you will if he's really a dragon, but it told me that you purchased it. Like I knew you were the ones that bought it too. Well, the mister was. You weren't around when she was given to a man by the name of Cooper Manning." She thought about what she sounded like, and was glad they didn't run her off. Yet, anyway. "The little one, uglier than the others, had some clay around it. I put that on there when she asked me to do it. I know this sounds like I'm off my noodle, but I swear to you, that's what she told me to do."

"I believe you." Toby was sure she could have hugged the man for saying that to her. But she didn't. There was trouble afoot, as her grannie said, and she needed to explain something to him. "Did it happen to tell you why you were to cover it up?"

"So that Donald the Asshole didn't know what he was putting out there. He would have stolen it too, had someone not, I'm assuming you, figured it out. But the pot told me that you were the one that was to get her. She said she talked to you before the auction." George asked her if she was hungry as they were headed to dinner. "I'm sorry. But I'm not wealthy or anything. I can't afford the places you're sure to go."

"Actually, I should have said that I'd pay." She looked back at her car, then at the man. "Is she with you? She can come with us as well. I'm sure you've talked to her about this."

"My grannie. And my son, Shawn Deaver. Grannie is my uncle's mom." Grannie got out of the car with Shawn and looked at herself in the car mirror before crossing the street. Shawn wouldn't have let go of Grannie's hand even if she begged him to. He loved her as much as Toby did. When someone nearly ran her down, she smacked the hood of their car and told them to slow the fuck down. "She's not at all what someone would think of when they think of a grandma. She's outspoken, rude at times, and has a mind of her own. But she's mine, and I love her to pieces. So does my son."

"This should be a very enjoyable meal then." As they were seated, Imp explained to her that they'd just gotten back from a much needed vacation. "It was only two days, but I feel as if I've been handed the world."

The chatter, what she thought of as small talk, wasn't boring. When Imp could, she included her grannie in the conversation and even asked them about where they were staying. Grannie had been warned not to tell people their situation. She might well have told her to tell her for all the good it did to ask Grannie to hush. Shawn sat in her lap when they were seated.

"Right now, we're staying in the car. Not as bad as it sounds. They're roomy seats, and we're not all that big. My son is an asshole. Both of them were, but Toby's dad, he's in prison. Jackass tried to rob one of them armored cars when it was just sitting at a light one day." Toby put her hand over her face and watched the reaction of the people she'd come to warn. Shawn pointed out that Grannie was going to have to be in time out. "When that pot called out to my Toby here, she said we'd have to go right then. Been three days sitting around waiting for one of you guys to show up. Now that you have, perhaps we'll hang around for a few days, make some money, and head on back. Toby, she's my lifeline. And that little fella of hers is hers."

"You're a very handsome young man, Shawn." Of course, just like he always did, he said he knew that. Imp laughed. "What is it you do for a living, Toby? Perhaps I can look for something to help you out while you're here."

"That won't be necessary. The pot asked me to tell you that someone is coming for it." The waitress came then and took their order for their meal. After ordering her food, thinking to share it with Shawn, Imp asked him what he wanted. As per his usual affair, when people risked asking a six-year-old what he wanted, he told her. "Shawn, these nice people don't want to pay for a steak when they've only just met us. Just order from the menu like a good boy."

"I'm having a steak too." After it was settled that George and Shawn were going to have a steak, medium rare, Grannie changed her order to a steak too. Toby stuck with her pasta meal and tried to get back to what she'd been sent here to do. "Toby, we're going to eat first. I know you have something to tell us, and I'm very happy that you've come here to tell us. But I'd like more than anything to just relax, enjoy a good meal, and then we'll go back to our home and talk. All right?"

"Can I get me a bath?" Toby was going to

find herself a deep hole and crawl to the bottom of it, hoping no one would look for her. But Imp told him that they had a really nice bathtub that he was more than welcome to use. "I have a couple of toys I play with at bath time. I didn't bring them all on account'a we're traveling light. Grannie said we had to bug out, but I was afraid that bugs were coming too, so Momma told me that we were just traveling light." He leaned over to Imp, and in his staged, very loud whisper, spoke again. "I don't know what that means either, but if Momma told me we'd be all right, I believed her."

"As you well should." She wasn't sure how it happened, but before their appetizers were brought to the table, Shawn was sitting between Imp and George, and she was enjoying her meal.

True to their word, they didn't speak of anything but the town, the things going on around town, as well as the things they'd been able to get done. Toby enjoyed herself. Grannie did as well, and when she asked if she could have a beer, Toby was almost glad they were going to the Manning home. Grannie was going to be snoring before they arrived, she'd bet.

Shawn finished his dinner before she did, but he stayed where he was. She knew he was getting sleepy. They'd not been sleeping all that well despite the large roomy seats. Not that he took a nap anymore, but he'd been cooped up for so long she knew it was exhausting him to be upset too.

Dessert was a bowl of sherbet for her, and Toby enjoyed some of it. Grannie didn't have any, but she did sample the cake that Imp had ordered. She noticed that neither of them drank coffee, and Imp drank juice. Whatever she was, Toby wasn't going to tangle with her. There was something very powerful about her.

By the time they were pulling into the Manning driveway, Toby was a nervous wreck. Grannie was sleeping, of course, and Toby was pinging off the walls again. She didn't blame him, really. To be able to be in a home and to burn off some of his never-ending energy was a good thing for everyone. As soon as they walked into the door, she backed the fuck up.

"That's a little person." Imp stood in front of her, telling her to breathe. "I can't. I can't breathe. It's a little person."

The slap to her face upset Shawn, but George was able to calm him down. When she was taken to the living room and sat on the couch, Toby looked around for more of the little creatures. Imp sat beside her and took her hand into hers.

"Will you tell me, or do I have to look?" She said she didn't like them. "It's more than that, and you know it. What happened that makes you so terrified of them? They're faeries and brownies here. Is it them, or just little people in general?"

Toby looked at the woman. "What are you? Tell me so that I know what I'm going to be dealing with when you call me a liar and toss me from your house." Imp said she was fae, but a great deal more. "I don't know what that might mean, but fae. That's what my son's father was. Not is, as I killed him, but he and his little minions kidnapped me, and he raped me over a four day period before I was able to kill him. I might die trying to kill you, but you'll not harm me or mine."

"I wouldn't anyway. You said you killed this fae. Do you know his name?" Toby shook her head. "All right. This is Velvet. She won't touch you unless you allow it. But she's going to be—"

"I'm not lying to you." Imp told her she knew that, and she knew that her fear was genuine. "When I went to the police station after I was able to get away, they arrested me. Of course, there wasn't a body for them to find, nor was there any evidence that I'd been at the house all that time. I have a hard time holding down a job because someone will hear my name and figure out what happened to me seven years ago. Why does Velvet want to touch me?"

"She can tell who it was that did this to you. Also, she can tell you how powerful he was. In that, it'll help you be able to deal with the magic Shawn already is showing signs of." She knew they'd seen it when his glass of milk refilled. Also, when he didn't have any catsup at the table quick enough for him to eat. "Will you allow her to do this for you?"

"I don't know what good it will do to know. I guess the magical stuff would be all right. But that's all. Nothing but a touch." Imp asked if she could touch Shawn instead if that made her feel better. "No. I don't want any of these things near my son."

"All right." When she put out her hand, Toby was ashamed that it was shaking. The little creature was very gentle with her touch, but it still made her want to scrub her hands until they were raw. She'd done that a great deal after getting away. The look on the little thing's face scared her a little. "Will she tell me too?"

"Of course. It's your right to know what sort of monster hurt you. Go on, Velvet, tell us what you were able to find out." The little person nodded, then looked at her before she spoke. "Is it bad, Velvet? I promise you that I won't hold it against you if it is."

"Nay, my lady. 'Tis not bad. Especially knowing he is dead. I am sorry that one of my kind hurt you so grievously, my lady." She looked at Imp. "He was Ames, my lady. The nephew to the king of the fae. Ames did just as she said, but Lady Toby hasn't told the whole story to anyone just as yet. The faeries and fae that have helped Ames have been dealt with by his father. It wasn't a good death for any of them."

"How do you know this if you've only touched me? Are you reading my mind?" Velvet told her that with the name, she knew what had happened. "I'm sorry. I didn't know anyone would have cared all that much once he was dead. I didn't know he was the son of the king or whatever he was either."

"Ames has been a terrible person since he was born. His mother is said to have overindulged him greatly when he was just a child. Then one day, he was to have gone away for the murder of one of the house faeries. The king was very angry at him, as it turned out, that he'd been murdering small ones since he'd been only a babe in his crib." Imp asked where the mother was now. "She is no more, my lady. Ames took her life when she agreed with the king that Ames needed to be put away. His mind, they all agreed, was not in a good spot."

"How the hell did he get away with what he did to me?" She hadn't realized she'd yelled until the faerie backed away. "It's not your fault. I know it's not anyone else's fault, but I've been blackballed for every job I've tried to get. We've moved so many times I can't remember my address anymore. All because of that fucking prick deciding I was going to be his plaything."

"It's not you, my lady, but the boy. There are people that wish to take him from you for what he is." She said he was her son. "And the grandson of the king of fae. He will need protection as his magic gets stronger. As it is now, it calls to the ones that wish him harm. Not only harm, Lady Toby, but they wish to bring his grandfather to heel for crimes against his son. Ames wasn't respected at all, but he was feared, and one of his last rules was to avenge his death. This was decreed long before he met and harmed you."

Not knowing what to do, she picked up Shawn when he came to her. The pajamas that he had on were like a pair he'd had at home. Holding her son tightly to her, she knew she couldn't do this on her own much longer. If she did, she was going to lose. She knew that.

"I need help." Velvet promised her that she'd have it. "While I think that's wonderful of you offering, even after the way I've treated you, I'm not sure what I can go up against magic that a king would have."

"Ah, but the king isn't after you, my lady. I will protect the three of you with my life."

The man standing in the room with her looked so much like Ames, or whatever his name was, that Toby screamed. The blackness that was coming up on her didn't just take her, but it slapped her around a couple of times before she finally was out. Whatever happened, she supposed she deserved it. That's what the cops had been telling her for years anyway.

Before You Go...

HELP AN AUTHOR

write a review

THANK YOU!

Share your voice and help guide other readers to these wonderful books. Even if it's only a line or two, your reviews help readers discover the author's books so they can continue creating stories that you'll love. Log in to your favorite retailer and leave a review. Thank you.

AWARD WINNING, BESTSELLING AUTHOR

Kathi Barton, a winner of the Pinnacle Book Achievement Award and a best-selling author on Amazon and All Romance books, lives in Nashport, Ohio, with her husband, Paul. When not creating new worlds and romance, Kathi and her husband enjoy camping and going to auctions. She can also be seen at county fairs with her husband, who is an artist and potter.

Her muse, a cross between Jimmy Stewart and Hugh Jackman, brings her stories to life for her readers in a way that has them coming back time and again for more. Her favorite genre is paranormal romance, with a great deal of spice. You can visit Kathi online and drop her an email if you'd like. She loves hearing from her fans. aaronskiss@gmail.com.

Follow Kathi on her blog: http://kathisbartonauthor.blogspot.com/

www.ingramcontent.com/pod-product-compliance
Lightning Source LLC
Chambersburg PA
CBHW020620180626
46810CB00007B/2866

9 781956 788648